THE GARGOYLE'S CAPTIVE

A DEAL WITH A DEMON

KATEE ROBERT

TRINKETS & TALES LLC

Map by Abigail M Larson

Edits by Manu Velasco

Copyedits by Tara Rayers

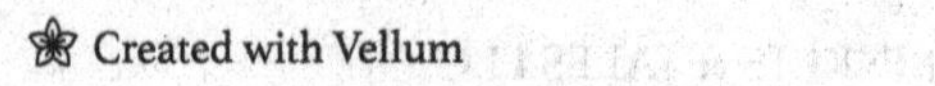

RUSALKA
THANE
INCUBI & SUCCUBI
KRAKEN
BARGAINER DEMONS
AZAZEL
DRAGON
BRAM
GARGOYLE
SOL

CONTENT NOTES

Some of the content of this book may be triggering for some readers. You can find the whole list of tropes, tags, and content warnings below. Reader discretion advised.

TROPES: Not-quite-enemies to lovers, monster romance

TAGS: Monster romance, monster hunter and her monster boyfriend, ribbed for her pleasure, every time you run I'll catch you and drag you to my bed, birth control pendant, who needs therapy when I have kinky sex?, trauma bonding, submissive monster, the reason we're uniquely suited for each other is the same reason we can never be together, demon deals, yes I lit you on fire and roasted a marshmallow on your (totally FINE) burning body but you are equally to blame, I tried to do this right but if you're going to lie to me then I'll be the monster you think I am, it's too big

CWs: elements of suicidal ideation (referenced briefly),

murder, blood, giant spiders, dubious consent (agreement given under duress), violent familial death (historical, off-page), abuse (by parents, off-page, historical), violence, blood magic

1
GRACE

"Let me out, you horned fucking monster!" I bang my fists on the door, but just like every other time, there's no answer. I knew this wasn't going to be easy, but I had no idea how difficult the damned demon was going to make it. I was under the impression that there was a time crunch, but he tossed me into this room as soon as he teleported me into the demon realm, and I haven't seen him—or anyone else—in the three days since. Well, there was a very exciting moment where a demon with horns in the place of eyes tattooed a sigil onto my skin that allows me to understand all the languages spoken in the demon realm. Ramanu was a chatty one but cryptic enough to make me want to pull out my hair. I was sorry to see them go, though. No matter how aggravating I found them, being with them was still better than being alone.

No one has come to my room since.

I turn from the door with a curse. My hands ache, but it's almost a relief because at least it's something *different*. I've already explored every inch of the luxurious, well-appointed bedroom. The mattress is the kind that invites you to sleep for a solid eight hours and then some, but I'm too stressed to catch up on the rest that I've been missing.

I hope Mina is okay.

I'm sure if the rest of my family were still alive, they'd have some comments about me being friends with . . . whatever Mina is. Vampire, yes. But something else too. I've never seen anyone with an aura like hers.

Azazel better have held up his end of the bargain. I gave him seven years of my life, and he saved the three vampires Mina's father took captive. I don't know the other two, but if Ryland is alive and well, he'll take care of Mina. That has to be enough.

For a monster hunter, lately I've been saving more of the so-called monsters than I've killed.

There's no use thinking about that, though. There's no use thinking of anything at all. I'm stuck, and yet I'm exactly where I want to be. I didn't expect to be locked in a room and left alone for days on end, but I'm in the demon realm now.

The same place my mother disappeared to, all those years ago. I even made a deal with the same demon, though I expected it to be easier to snoop around for the answers I seek. Azazel certainly didn't seem interested in offering them up when I first asked.

Time passes, but I can't begin to guess how much. The sun rises and sets outside my window, and people move about their day, but surely there are more hours in a day here than back home. There must be, because time stretches like taffy while I'm stuck here. My meals seem to show up at regular intervals, but the fare, while delicious, is difficult to identify. Maybe demons don't categorize their meals into breakfast, lunch, and dinner the same way so many humans do. Impossible to say.

I'm closer to answers than I've ever been, and yet finding them feels like an impossible task.

I can't pick the lock. I gave up trying after the dozenth time I got it unlocked and then it locked again before I could turn the knob. There's some magic at play, but this place is the equivalent of an enchanted castle, so of course there is.

I'm sitting on the bed, shredding one of the many dresses I found in the wardrobe, when the door opens and the demon himself appears.

Azazel is a big fucker. He's got to be well over seven feet tall when one accounts for his horns, great curving black things that bring a bull to mind. His shoulders fill the doorway, and despite myself, a little shiver of fear works through me. Somewhere, some scholar of the Bible must have had an interaction with a bargainer demon like Azazel when they started crafting their depiction of the devil. His crimson skin is otherworldly, and while his face isn't exactly unattractive by human standards, it is decidedly *not* human.

He crosses his arms over his massive chest and looks down at the mess I've made. "If you're thinking of tying those together and scaling out a window, I'm going to disabuse you of the idea. Not only are we too far off the ground for you to make it down safely, but there are carnivorous winged creatures that hunt the skies in these parts."

Truth be told, I don't actually have a plan for the dress. It just helps to stay in motion. Not that I'm about to tell him that. "Considering that the deal I signed says I can't come to harm, I'm surprised you let those creatures flock around your precious castle."

"On the contrary, I find their presence incredibly useful. They keep the gargoyles, the incubi, and the succubi from getting any ideas. My people don't generally fly, and so the skies are a potential weak point."

I search his aura for a lie, but it's only the deep yellow of amusement threaded with the deep forest green of pride that always seems to be there. He's laughing at me. *Bastard*. I force myself not to drop the fabric. Instead, I tear another strip. "If I knew I was agreeing to such a boring seven years, I would've insisted on including some additional clauses in the contract."

No use thinking about the contract now. It does, in fact, promise my safety and that I won't be forced into doing anything that would cause me harm. It also has a clause that spells out exactly what would happen to any child I have here in the demon realm. *That* sure as shit isn't going to happen, though.

Azazel steps into the room fully, and the door shuts behind him as if blown by a strong wind. I jump. He doesn't. He just gives me a long look. "Tonight, there will be an auction. The leaders of the other four territories will come here, and each of them will choose one of my humans to be their companion for the next seven years. There will be a secondary contract in place that reinforces everything you already agreed to."

I stare at him for several beats. "Why are you telling me this?"

"Because you're Grace Jaeger. I know what your family does, and I know what you're capable of. So I'm going to be explicit with you, right here, right now. If you kill, maim, or otherwise harm a single being in the demon realm, your contract will be null and void. Should that happen, I will stick you out on the roof of my castle and allow the hunters in the sky to eat you at their leisure."

My shiver of fear becomes a full-on tremor. "Do you normally threaten the humans you make bargains with?"

"No." His expression gives nothing away. "Only the ones who come from a family whose reputation warns of the atrocities they've committed against nonhumans."

The comment stings more because he's not wrong. I may only go after monsters who have already harmed a human, but my grandparents? My great-grandparents? My great-great-grandparents? Add as many "greats" as you want—the further back in history we go, the less the Jaegers cared about what really made a monster. For them, it was less action and more bloodline. I read the journals. I know exactly how fucked up it was. "I wouldn't do that."

"All the same. I want there to be no misunderstanding between us. Too much is resting on the next seven years, and I won't have anyone endangering my people."

I bite back my instinctive response. He's not technically being unfair, no matter how frustrating I find this conversation. "I won't hurt anyone who doesn't fuck with me first." When Azazel just stares, I curse and clarify. "I won't hurt anyone who doesn't... hurt me first. That's as good as it's going to get."

"If someone harms you, *I* will be the one to take care of it." The way he says this indicates the conversation is over. He motions at the wardrobe. "I need you dressed to impress tonight."

There's a part of me that wants to defy him out of sheer spite, but the truth is that I entered the contract of my own free will. Throwing a hissy fit now serves no one, and would be, frankly, embarrassing. "I would like to know what happened to my mother." It's the same question I asked him right after he teleported me here.

"No, you wouldn't." Without another word, he turns

around and walks out of the room. Again, the door swings shut with a force just short of slamming. I'd love to blame Azazel for that, but I was watching him walk away when it happened. He never touched it.

Sometimes I fucking hate magic.

Even my own; especially my own. Because, before Azazel turned around and walked away, his aura shifted to a pale blue that I am all too familiar with. *Sorrow*.

Just like that, I know my mother's dead.

I want to say it's exactly what I expected. She made a deal with a demon and never came home. I've been operating on the assumption that I'm an orphan for years now. It's just that . . . after I saw the contract, a small part of me wanted to believe that maybe she had chosen to stay in the demon realm for some unknown reason. That maybe she was still alive. That maybe I'm not really the last of my family.

I knew better, but apparently that hopeful little child who misses her mama hasn't quite died of sorrow yet. Or at least she hadn't until she saw that same emotion reflected in Azazel's aura.

I go through the motions of getting dressed. There's no point in defying the order. I have a feeling I'll be dragged out to the auction no matter what I choose to wear, and my pride isn't dead yet.

I find a purple dress that'll serve my purpose, and I even take the time to put some cosmetics on my face. They're an identifiable brand, which means they're imported from the human realm. How thoughtful.

Exactly two hours after Azazel left, my door opens softly. A clear invitation. It's all I've wanted for days on end, and yet I find myself reluctant to walk through. There's no going back after this. The thought almost makes me laugh. There was no going back from the moment I signed the contract.

No, we can trace the line of this even further back, to when I heard Azazel's name on Mina's lips. Or even further, to when my mother made the demon deal in the first place, leaving behind only a note with the barest details.

There's never been any other choice but to take that first step and walk out of my room. I'm not remotely surprised to find four others in the hallway. I take them in at a glance, but ultimately they matter less than what happens next. None of them look like me, like a hunter. They're just normal people. I don't know if that's comforting or terrifying.

In the end, it makes no difference. I turn and stalk in the direction that feels best, distantly aware of the fact that they follow, little ducklings led to the slaughter. Except not a slaughter. Just because my mother died doesn't mean Azazel's bargains are bullshit. My life would be simpler if they were. There would be fewer questions keeping me up at night.

Around me, I feel the magic of the castle moving. The sensation was more muted when I was in my room, which confirms what I suspected: there were spells as well as walls locking me in. This is an honest-to-gods enchanted castle. *Charming*.

The castle finally spits us through a door that leads to a large room. The lights are all aimed at our faces, but as I move to the short dais, I catch sight of scales, tentacles, and wings. Monsters. And not the kind you find back in the human realm. We are so far removed from the bloodlines that run through the beings here that most of our monsters don't look any different from the rest of humanity, at least most of the time. I have a feeling the ones in this room are currently as human as they're capable of looking.

Before the realms split and crossing them became all but impossible, these were the types of creatures my ancestors hunted.

Maybe the thought should fill me with some kind of purpose or generational rage, but all I feel is tired. My head is too full of the color blue to worry about a past that stretches generations before my birth.

I thought I was done mourning my mother. It took so long before I gave up hope that she was ever coming back, and I knew better than to rekindle that feeling when I found Azazel. And yet here I am, feeling just as lost as I was at twenty.

I bury the feeling down deep, shove it into a little box, and wrap it in chains before I toss it into the darkest corner of myself. I am surrounded by predators, and I cannot afford to be distracted. I've been promised safety, but the contract specifies consequences for harm—not magical protection from it.

I'm so distracted, I don't realize the auction has started. If "auction" is even the right word. The few that I've attended have multiple bidding scenarios, and for this one, they are simply speaking of colors . . . Oh. *Oh*. The colors of our dresses. I hear someone say purple—what I'm wearing—but the lights are too bright for me to identify who has claimed me.

I can see their auras, though.

There's plenty of red anger and the sickly yellow green with a hint of brown that is hate. These beings don't like each other. But more worrying is the bright pink of lust threading through the entire room. These monsters want us. There may be language in the contract that prevents us from being forced into any kind of intimate situation, but if we're sent off, out of Azazel's watchful eye, who will be there to enforce it?

I can defend myself... probably.

But what about the others?

Even as I look down the line of us, noting the fear on many of the other four's faces, in their all-too-human auras, the lights shift. Azazel moves with purpose, and what comes next happens almost faster than I can follow. Each of us is shuttled to a different door that I'm certain wasn't there before. I get a better look at the monsters.

A dragon. A kraken. A being who looks almost human, except for their size, smoky skin, long tail, the coal-black claws on their hands, and their cloven hooves. So, really, not that human at all. And, finally, one who looks even more human. They're big too. They're *all* big. The shadows shift, and I pick out their massive wings and two pairs of horns peeking out of their white hair.

They're looking right at me.

2

BRAM

There's a flavor to desperation that I've become all too familiar with, and it soaks into every inch of this space. All us leaders are feeling it in our own way though each of us would die before we'd admit it. Sol, the dragon, feels backed into a corner, but there's a cautious hope in his energy that sticks in my throat. Thane, the kraken, flat out doesn't want to be here at all. And Rusalka . . . Well, there's no desperation in *her* energy, just a deep anticipation that worries me.

I don't want to be beholden to Azazel.

Unfortunately, I don't have a fucking choice.

None of my people will have me. Not with the curse hanging over my head, courtesy of my father's poor decisions. I've exhausted the suitable candidates in the other noble families. They don't want to join their houses to mine, even if it means any children produced will rule the territory after me. Not when they are so sure the curse will take their lives long before they take leadership.

Which is why I'm here, sitting in the castle of my enemy, acting as if everything is fine. Oh, I know Azazel is significantly better than his predecessor, but that doesn't mean I'll ever forgive or forget what he's responsible for. It wasn't *his predecessor* who made the bargain with my father that ended with my family dead. Even without that element of blame, it wasn't too long ago that the entire demon realm was at war and I was doing my damnedest to kill the very people who sit so casually in this room with me.

Azazel knew how to bait his trap well.

And it *is* a trap. He's too canny to do anything out of the goodness of his heart, which means he has half a dozen plots in play, and they all center around the five human women standing on the dais. Are they plants? Spies? Even assassins? By the time we find out, it will be too late.

I should leave.

Except I don't have a damned choice.

All the women are beautiful and all just as likely to be my downfall. They'll have to get in line behind the nobles in my territory and Fate, which seems determined to kick me when I'm down. Repeatedly.

I have only one route forward. A bargain and a human companion.

I grit my teeth and examine the women a little more closely. Pale skin. Tan skin. Blonde, brunette, redhead. Beautifully fat and lean and in-between. Human, every one.

Despite myself, my attention snags on the tall dark-haired woman in purple. Unlike the others, she stares out at the room with a provocation that feels almost violent. With the lights positioned as they are, there's no way she can see the details of us, but that doesn't stop her from challenging us with her dark eyes. It feels like she reaches across the distance and hooks her nails right into my chest.

She's a terrible choice. I need someone docile and submissive. Someone who won't make waves, who won't drive away the few allies I have left in my territory. Someone like the shivering redhead or the smiling voluptuous brunette in blue.

But when I open my mouth, the word I speak is . . . "They're all the same to me." Lies. I'm a godsdamned liar. "Purple."

Azazel gives me a short look that I can't define, but nods. I barely pay attention as the rest of the auction wraps up, one leader after the other claiming one of the humans as their own. Doors appear around the perimeter of the room, and each pair is guided into one of them. There will be a contract to negotiate the finer details. Again, Azazel proves his cleverness by not giving us time to linger near the other leaders. He says he wants peace, and his actions seem to indicate he's telling the truth—at least on the surface. I know better than to trust that, though.

The room we're left waiting in is just big enough for me to spread my wings. I resist the urge. The last thing I need is Azazel thinking he made me nervous, even if it's true. Instead, I watch the woman.

She paces from one corner of the room to the other, her long legs eating up the distance in smooth strides. She's more muscular than I realized, her lean strength on full display in her fitted purple dress. Like the others, she's beautiful—but hers is the kind of beauty one finds in the hellcats that haunt the succubi and incubi's territory. Gorgeous and deadly and all too willing to eat your face off.

There isn't a sliver of fear present in her energy either. Just the burnt orange of irritation. I don't know if that's a relief or something to worry about. To the best of my knowledge, these humans are new to this realm and have been kept mostly isolated from the bargainer demons. She should be shocked or scared or *something* to be faced with all of us.

There must be some reasonable explanation. "Are you a witch?"

She snorts. "Hardly."

I should stop talking, should wait for Azazel to arrive. Until the contract is signed, there's every chance that the whole deal can be called off. But I find myself shifting so she'll look at me again. "You're taking this whole thing rather well."

"I made a deal with a demon. Compared to Azazel, you're just a dude with bat wings. Nothing to write home about." She smirks. "Cute horns, though. Really adorable."

My horns are not *adorable*.

I have to fight the instinctive urge to touch them. She's gotten under my skin in a matter of seconds, which doesn't bode well for the next seven years. I may not have wanted this, but I vowed to myself that I would be charming and kind. The contract allows for me to do my best to seduce my new human partner into giving me the one thing I need above all else. A child.

But I'm already fighting the urge to snarl instead of smile, to snap instead of seduce. I am well and truly fucked.

Before I can do something foolish, the door opens and Azazel walks in. He pauses for the briefest moment, almost as if he expected to find bloodshed, and then moves to a desk that appeared the second the door opened. I feel the magic of the castle gather to provide what he needs, but I'm intrigued that the human doesn't seem surprised by it.

Again, I'm certain she's had exposure to magic before.

Again, I wonder if this is all an elaborate trap.

I have no illusions about my position. I'm the weakest of the current leaders. The others may not realize how precarious my position is in this moment, but Azazel does. His knowledge was there in his carefully worded invitation. He knew I couldn't say no, and he knew why.

He folds his giant hands and stares at us over his black claws. "I have reservations about this pairing. I would like to give each of you this opportunity to change your mind, with the understanding that if neither of you *does* change your mind, you'll be signing a contract that will attach the two of you for the next seven years." Before I can cut in and say things are fine, he pins her with a severe look. "There is no wiggle room. You are safe from harm, but that clause extends to *your* harming *others*. I won't have you going on a rampage in my realm."

Curiosity flares, but I can't let that comment stand. "It's not your realm, Azazel."

"No," he agrees easily. Too easily. "But if any of the territory leaders abuses my gift, that could change rather quickly. Which leads me to my next point." He studies me far too intently. Bargainer demons hold their powers close, keeping their secrets, but I'm nearly 100 percent certain they don't hold the same magic that my people do. Which means he can't see my emotions swirling around me. Not like I can see his.

Which is right around the moment that I realize he's being . . . genuine? There's no calculation there. Only the neutral gray of worry.

"I'm listening."

"I am aware of your history and the complications that this sort of circumstance will bring you. I extended this offer as a courtesy so you weren't the only one left out of negotiations, but I want your word that your history will not factor into how you treat my human."

"Oh, fuck off with that noise." The human in question props her hands on her hips and glares. It's honestly impressive that she doesn't seem scared of him in the least. Especially when he's three times her size and she barely comes up to his shoulder. "You know damned well that I'm more than capable of taking care of myself."

"That's not the point." He turns that severe expression on her, and it's a testament to her strength that she doesn't wilt in the least. A hint of exasperation feathers through him, and it's almost like she can see it too, because her lips quirk just a little.

I don't know if I should step in or just watch this play out. There's something going on here beyond what I expected. Bargainer demons are notoriously protective of their humans, so I expected Azazel to threaten me to ensure my good behavior. It's not necessary, though. I need this human, unexpected or not.

Her smile, such as it is, drops away. "I gave you my word, Azazel. More, I signed that damned contract. If it's as good as you claim it is, you have nothing to worry about."

I'm not sure if she's saying it to reassure him . . . or to threaten him. From the worry that strengthens in the air around him, he's not sure either. Under other circumstances, I would be wholly entertained to see this demon, who's been a royal pain in my ass for decades, set back on his heel so effectively. But this isn't another circumstance. I need him not to go back on this bargain.

I shift, flaring my wings out the slightest bit to draw their attention to me. "As entertaining as this is, if we're going to make a bargain, let's sign the contract and be done with it."

For a moment, I think Azazel might call the whole thing off. Instead, he shakes his head slowly. "Very well. As discussed, there will be regular check-ins with a demon of my choosing. If at any point the contract is violated, the gargoyle territory becomes mine. There are several clauses to ensure good behavior from all parties."

"Yes, yes, we've gone over it." She motions impatiently. "I'm hungry, tired, and the last thing I want to do is continue circling this subject with both of you. Give me the pen and I'll sign."

"You should read over the contract."

She doesn't. She just plucks the pen from his hand and scrawls her name on the appropriate line. *Grace*. A pretty name, light and ethereal . . . and nothing like the woman standing next to me.

Her impatience batters away at me, but I have too much history with bargainer demons to sign a contract without reading it through one last time. Azazel sent over a copy for us to study before attending this auction, but I'd be a fool to assume there were no edits made between then and now.

Sure enough, there is a clause that's been added halfway through. I read it and then read it again. I glance at Azazel with raised brows. His only answer to my unspoken question is a tight nod. Still, I can't help asking, "Were the same edits made to all the contracts?"

"No."

Who *is* this woman? Or was this clause about her not being able to harm anyone in my territory added because of what happened with my father? A horrible little voice whispers in the back of my mind: *If she kills me, then at least I won't have to worry about anything any longer. It will finally be over.* I shrug and sign in the appropriate place.

"With that, I'll leave you to it. Your first check-in will be sometime this week. I expect you to extend the same courtesy to Ramanu that you would to any member of your court."

I've bent over backward to please my court, twisting

myself up in knots to try—and ultimately fail—to earn their goodwill and trust. To combat years of my father's rule that ate away at both until there was nothing left. It's no small miracle that I'm even able to rule at all, though that's less a testament of my skill and more proof that my people are scared enough of the curse to steer clear of me. For now.

An impossible situation. That's nothing new, though. I've been fighting my way uphill, inch by inch, for years. I won't be able to make further headway until I have an heir who lives to see their majority and convince my people the curse is broken, but at least I have a path forward to that outcome.

I just need to convince this strange, potentially dangerous human to bear my child. Somehow, I think all the impossible hurdles I've cleared to date will be nothing compared to this challenge.

3

GRACE

I think I made an error. My nerves are starting to get the best of me, and the hint of sorrow that flickers through Azazel every time he looks at me makes it almost unbearable to be in his presence. I just want this over with. The gargoyle—Bram—is an unknown, but unless I am spectacularly unlucky, he won't have a magic castle that will lock me in. I should be able to pick any normal lock.

It's not that I intend to break my word. Just bend it a little.

I want to know what happened to my mother. If she's dead, and all evidence points to that being the case, it happened here in the demon realm despite Azazel's promise of safety. Ideally, I would have the whole of the bargainer demon territory to the answers Azazel is keeping from me. As it is, I'll have to slip my gargoyle captor and make my way back here on my own.

I don't plan to *stay* gone, of course. As soon as I have my answers, I'll honor my word and play companion to the bat-man.

Hardly an ideal situation, but I've been dealing with

impossible situations for years now. Being the last monster hunter from one of the most famous monster-hunting families in the human realm means I'm the one people call when they have no one else.

For the first time, guilt flickers through me. I was also thinking about myself when I agreed to pay the price for Mina's bargain. I needed answers, and the demon realm is where they live.

I'm only now considering the potential implications of me being absent for seven years. There are other monster hunters. But few of them have been around as long as the Jaegers. They don't have the track record, the trust, or the word of mouth that gives people a place to turn.

This should've been something I considered before saying yes. Or, at the very least, I should have negotiated some leniency about returning to the human realm to take care of any emergencies. I straighten my spine. It's too late for regrets. I have to deal with the situation I've made. Besides, I may have signed the contract just now, but there's nothing to say I can't request an amendment to it.

Except . . . I don't.

Azazel rolls the contract up. I don't make any suggestions as Bram turns for the door and motions for me to follow him. I don't speak a single word as we walk down the hall that certainly wasn't there before to a grand arched door that has plenty of room to fit Bram's wings through.

Bram glances sideways at me. "Are you afraid of heights?"

It's an effort not to roll my eyes. The only reason I resist is because I need him to trust me enough to not post a guard on me every hour of every day. As it is, his aura is almost completely the burnt orange of irritation. I'm sure there's some way to garner goodwill, but at this point, I just want to be left alone. "No."

"This should be a memorable experience then." Without another word, he scoops me into his arms. I'm so shocked at his audacity that I don't immediately fight him. Or at least that's what I tell myself. By the time I realize I *should* be fighting him, he opens the door and sweeps through . . . into nothingness.

I don't scream. One of the first lessons a Jaeger learns is to be silent in response to fear. A scream or even a whimper can get you killed when you're on the hunt.

But I sure as shit cling to Bram as he launches himself through the air, seemingly miles above the ground. The cold cuts through my insufficient dress as if it were nothing. That's the only reason I huddle against his broad chest. Not because it feels nice to be held by him. Our hair whips around us violently enough to cut skin.

I think Bram laughs though I can't be sure because the wind whisks away any sound. I can't even focus properly to check his aura. *Bastard.* He did this on purpose.

I can't speak. I can't fight for fear of falling. I can't do anything as we wing our way through the air. The hopelessness of the situation closes around my throat, making me want to hurt him. It's everything I can do to stay still.

We seem to fly forever. Misery, along with the cold, sears its way to my very bones. I'm certain I'll never be warm again. I've endured torture sessions less agonizing than this experience.

When Bram gathers me close, I forget myself enough to just be grateful for a little extra warmth. At least until his voice sounds in my ear. "Brace yourself."

I don't get a chance to ask him what I'm bracing myself for. The bastard pulls his wings together, and then we're diving toward the ground at mind-bending speed. Still, I don't scream. I didn't think I'd go out like this, crushed in a million pieces, but I suppose they are worse ways to die.

I can't open my eyes, and even if I could manage, I wouldn't be able to see past the tears caused by the wind. I barely notice that our horrifying dive has turned into something slightly more controlled when the angle of our bodies changes. We're still moving too fast, but I think we're parallel to the ground again.

Bram backwings, and my stomach tries to keep moving in the previous direction. If I whimper, the sound is lost. Or at least I hope it is. He lands almost gracefully, and then —*finally*—we're no longer moving.

"You can open your eyes now." His body shifts as he walks, and even if my pride hates it, the reality is that if he sets me down now, I'll collapse in a pathetic heap. "We'll have to get you more appropriate clothing for the next time. I forgot how fragile humans are. So sensitive to temperature."

"I am never doing that again." I already have a disadvantage on the ground against monsters. I may have inherited the ability to see auras like the rest of the Jaegers, but the rest of me is human. I wasn't born with superior strength or stamina. Everything I have, I had to fight for. When it comes to battle, I will always be outclassed. It's why I fight dirty. At least in the human realm, technology can give me an edge and make up for my lack of physicality. Here, that's not an option.

I fight against my body's instinctive desire to curl in on itself. Opening my eyes is the first step. It proves to be a mistake, because Bram's face is so close to mine. He really is a handsome fucker. His features look a little like someone hacked them out of a mountain, rough and almost unfinished in some ways. It's more appealing than I'll ever admit. His jaw looks strong enough to take a punch and then some, more likely to break the attacker's hand than to yield.

And his skin . . .

Without thinking, I reach up and touch his jaw. He's warm, yes, but his skin doesn't feel like skin. It feels like stone. Smooth and movable, but stone nonetheless. Getting through it with any kind of blade would be impossible. It would take some kind of crushing weapon, like a mace or a hammer. Even then, the strength required? Impossible for me.

Not that I plan on killing this gargoyle.

I signed a contract, after all. Plus, he might've just scared the shit out of me, but he hasn't actually hurt me or anyone else to the best of my knowledge. If I go around killing monsters simply because they're monsters, then I'm no better than my ancestors. But I am a Jaeger. I can't help the way my brain works.

Maybe that's why I ask the question simmering in the front of my mind. "Can you burn?"

He eyes me. His eyes aren't blue or gray or any color I've ever seen. They look almost violet in the current light. Or whatever the nearly white shade of purple would be called. I'm no artist.

I might be embarrassed to be staring so intently if he wasn't doing the exact same thing. He studies my face as if he's never seen a human before. Maybe he hasn't. They don't seem that common in this realm.

Or maybe he's horrified that I just asked him if he burns.

"No," he finally says. He's already on the move, carrying me across what I realize is a roof. It's made of stone and looks like the newer version of some of the castles I've seen in Europe. I try to crane my head to see over the half wall thing that keeps folks without wings from walking right off the edge.

"I can walk."

"You're saying that out of pride. If I put you down, you're going to buckle like a newborn babe. It will waste both our time."

He's not wrong, but that doesn't stop me from resenting him for speaking it out loud. My body has finally started to realize that we're not going to freeze to death, and little tremors work through my muscles, making me twitch uncontrollably. I'm pathetically grateful for the warmth of Bram's body.

I resent that gratitude, too.

He takes me through an archway nearly identical to the one we used to leave the bargainer demons' castle. Except this one doesn't actually have a door attached. He walks down what feels like an endless number of stairs, and I can't help noticing that the stairs curve around a circular shaft that's plenty deep for me to fall to my death. Obviously, those with wings prefer not to use the staircase.

Again, I am grateful Bram isn't flying us to our destination within the castle. Again, I resent that feeling of gratitude. I don't know this gargoyle, and I don't plan to stick around for long enough to change that. Each time I appreciate him is just another sticky string making it more challenging to slip out without warning.

We go down what I think translates to two more levels and into a wide, high hallway. There are a handful of arches on either side, and I get a glimpse into the rooms as we pass. They seem normal enough, at least by human standards.

What the fuck am I thinking?

I'm not in the human realm. If I keep comparing everything I find here to that, I'm no better than some prejudiced asshole. I might not be here to learn about these people or live with them in any true way, but that doesn't mean I have to be a dick about it.

Besides, it will be easier to escape the castle if people aren't watching me closely because I keep insulting everything about them. Which means I should probably stop touching this man and asking him leading questions about his vulnerabilities. I have no intention of fighting him, setting him on fire, or committing any other kind of violence. Not unless I have to.

He finally sets me down carefully in front of the door at the end of the hallway. His big hands linger on my hips, and for the life of me, I can't tell if it's because he likes touching me, or if he really does think I might collapse. It doesn't matter, because neither of those things is going to happen. I take a small step back, and Bram releases me instantly.

It's probably the first step in an intricate dance he intends to conduct. Maybe even a seduction. That's too damned bad. Even if he is big and handsome and incredibly warm. I take another step back, mostly for my peace of mind. The air of the hallway is significantly more temperate than outside, but it's hardly balmy. Now that he's no longer touching me, I can't help shivering in cold.

He motions at the door behind me. "Your room is through there. There are some clothes available, but I'll have others made after we get your measurements. Dinner is in an hour." He pauses, as if realizing how brusque he sounds. "I would appreciate it if you would eat with me."

Spending more time with him is the last thing I want to do, but I'm not going to give him a reason to watch me closely. I'll have dinner with him tonight, and after the rest of the castle is asleep, I'll slip out and make my way back to the bargainer demon territory to find the answers I'm seeking. We didn't fly for days on end so I can't be more than a week's travel. Maybe. I need to find a map to verify before I start out, so maybe leaving tonight isn't the best idea. I'll have to see what I can source between now and dinner and then decide based on that.

No. Damn it, I'm stalling. It doesn't matter. I've lived off the land before, and even if the bargainer demon territory is a couple hundred miles away, I can make the trek. I only agreed to stay in this realm. Everything else is up for grabs.

I hate the uncomfortable guilt that rises. I'll come back. No doubt Azazel will be only too happy to ferry me to Bram once I get my answers. And that's *fine*. I said I'd stay here for seven years, and I will, but that damned demon knows what happened to my mother and I can't stand being this close without finding out the truth.

I look up at Bram. "Dinner would be great."

4

BRAM

There's something off about Grace's energy, but I can't quite put my finger on what. All the other people in the demon realm, regardless of who they call their own, experience the same emotions. It always shows up exactly alike: deep ocean blue for contentment, red for anger, a rich green for jealousy. The energy around Grace feels muted, as if she's drawn into herself. That sort of thing shouldn't be possible. I suspect it has more to do with how she processes her emotions than any kind of mysterious magic she's conducting.

Still, it means she's hiding something.

Perhaps I should let it go. I don't imagine humans make deals with bargainer demons when their lives are perfect and well-adjusted. I want to build something between us on trust, to convince her to share my bed long enough to conceive a child and then carry it to term. That won't happen if I start accusing her of lying to me within an hour of bringing her here.

But I'm not a fool.

The other people in this realm might think humans are

the weak ones, playthings to be passed around or bargained for, but I know exactly how dangerous they really are. Gods, one of the first full sentences Grace spoke to me was to ask if I can burn. That's not a normal thing to think. I just hope Grace isn't as bloodthirsty as . . .

No. I'm not going to think about that. This is as close to a fresh start as I can get, and it's vital I take advantage of it. I won't get another chance. Besides, Azazel snuck in that clause preventing her from harming me or my people. I'm not exactly certain how it will be enforced, but bargainer demon magic is a strange, fluid thing.

I leave her be and head to make arrangements for dinner. There aren't many people about, but then there are never many people about these days. The noble families ensure there are enough of them in residence to be properly represented, but their absence leaves the court feeling like a ghost town. I still remember the time when I couldn't walk down the halls without seeing half a dozen people, when our dinners and events were filled wall-to-wall, when we needed a full staff at all times to ensure everyone's needs were met.

That was a long time ago.

I only see one person as I head down to the main floor, and they duck into a side hallway before I can identify them. It's always like this. People scurry out of my way as if even a brush with my shadow is enough to transfer my family curse to them. There was never actually a real curse in play. Just a series of shitty decisions with fatal consequences. Not that they know or care about that.

In the kitchen, I find an unfamiliar person making biscuits. "Who are you?" He seems to know his way around the space, but I don't remember hiring anyone. "Where is the cook? Where is . . ." I trail off, realizing I don't remember the name of the most recent cook. They were good at their job and made really excellent bread, but I had only hired them a few weeks ago. Gods, what is their name?

"Jay quit." The man finishes cutting the biscuits and places them on a metal tray. "Before they left, they hired me as their replacement."

I stare at him for several beats. "You have to know that's not the usual sequence of events." Though I don't know if there *is* a normal sequence of events these days. I've been hemorrhaging staff for years, barely able to retain enough people on the payroll to keep this place running. Jay isn't the first cook to disappear without a word, but they are the first to hire a replacement before they did.

"It's a job." He shrugs. "I'm aware of the rumors around you and this place, but Jay said this job comes with pay, room, and board. And that the pay was good."

My father had a firm belief that everything was up for negotiation, and he seemed to enjoy haggling with the staff about their wages. I don't have the luxury. I study this man. He's on the lean side, a good head and shoulders shorter than me, and his skin has more of a blue tinge to it than purple. Nothing about his appearance tells me anything useful.

"What did Jay tell you the wages are?"

He rattles off a number that has me gritting my teeth. It's nearly double what I actually paid Jay. At this point, though, the new cook has me over a barrel whether he knows it or not. I drag my hand over my face. My father will be rolling in the grave over what I say next, but I wouldn't be in this position if it weren't for his poor choices, so fuck him. "If you stay past the first month, I'll double them."

He raises his brows and shifts his wings restlessly. "The initial wages are already borderline robbery."

"True, but that won't stop you from taking them, or taking the raise after a month." If he stays that long.

He runs his hand through his short black hair. "I'm not as superstitious as the rest of our people. If the pay is good and no one fucks with me, I'm more than happy to stay in the kitchen and collect my income."

"That's very enlightened of you."

He shrugs again. "No, not really. Anyone with a little bit of brainpower would realize that if there *is* a curse, it only affects you and your family. You're not looking to marry a lowly cook, so I should be in no danger."

I don't know if I should be depressed or relieved, but at this point, I'm out of options. "I'll need dinner prepared for me and my . . ." I'm not sure what to call Grace. She's a guest, but a guest who stays for seven years is practically a resident. I barely know the woman, so calling her my partner or anything more intimate doesn't make sense or feel right. "Lady," I finally finish awkwardly.

"I already started. Dinner will be served in an hour." He turns back to the oven, then glances over his shoulder at me. "My name is Silas by the way."

I nod and leave the kitchen as quickly as possible. It seems like every time I turn around, something else is going wrong. I'm flying through a storm, getting buffeted back and forth by unexpected winds, certain to be struck by lightning at any moment. There's only one way to fix this, and I don't know if I'm up to the task.

If not for the fact that my absence would plunge my territory into a civil war, I would've stepped down as territory leader years ago. I'm the last of my family. That means that without me in the picture, any belief about a curse should dwindle away to nothing. Someone else could step into this position easily enough . . . if not for the politics involved. My family has ruled our territory for as far back as anyone can remember. While we have married the other noble families into our ranks, there's always been someone from our line to inherit the title.

Until now.

For once in my fucking life, I want nothing more than to be selfish, but fear of the cost haunts me. If I fail, if war comes, not only will hundreds—if not thousands—die in the infighting, but our territory will be so weakened that it will take no effort at all for one of the others to sweep in and finish us off.

No, I have to succeed. I have no other choice.

I can't think inside these walls. This is my childhood home, and there once was a time when I ran through these halls with the confidence that nothing and no one could touch me. That I was perfectly safe. Now this place is more like a mausoleum. A memory of all I've lost that I can never escape. If I stop moving, it feels like the walls are closing in. Almost as if they will press me into mortar and stone, course over me until I am no longer a man, until I'm just another ghost haunting these hallways.

The dark thoughts drive me to the nearest vertical shaft and push me to launch myself into the air. I clear the castle walls in seconds, and only then can I breathe properly. At least for a moment. But everywhere I look is more evidence of what will be lost if I'm not skilled enough to succeed.

The peaks to the north, across the large lake, butt up against Rusalka's territory. She already has her fiery fingers sunken into plenty of people in my territory. The delights she offers are intense enough to combat their instinctive fear of both incubi and succubi. My people only remember how brutal the last war was when it's convenient for them.

If I keep flying, over the mountains to the west and past

the bargainer demon territory to the ocean, I could just go until my wings give out and I plummet into the water. There would be no curse to worry about then. Maybe the memories plaguing me would finally cease rattling around in the back of my mind where I can never escape.

The look of surprise on my father's face, frozen there in death.

My sister's blood soaking the stones as her breath rattles to a stop.

The twins, their bodies so badly damaged that I'm not even certain what killed them. Only who.

The knowledge that I ran when I should have fought, that I hid when I should have helped.

I *should* have died that day with the rest of my family. Every moment I've lived since then feels stolen. That's the true curse I live under.

The claustrophobic feeling inside me presses hard until I want to rip my skin off just to be rid of it. I know I need to keep everything inside, to power through any sign of weakness, but it bubbles up despite my best effort.

I throw my head back and keen my grief to the wind.

5

GRACE

I'm leaning halfway out my window, examining the exterior of the castle for a backup exit route, when I see the distant form of Bram shooting into the air. I pause despite myself. I was never one to wish for wings or flight. Being able to read people's auras is magic enough, though no one really talks about how horrific it is that you can't be lied to. Why wish for more? It seems to me that all magic is a double-edged blade, and I'm sure flight is no different.

It certainly is beautiful to watch, though. Bram cuts through the air the way sharks swim through the sea, every bit of energy seemingly devoted to his mobility, his speed. At least until he arches, throwing his head back. Even at this distance, I hear his cry and feel an answering twinge in my chest. I don't need to see the white edged with pale blue pulsing from his body to know that he's experiencing grief on a level most people can only dream of.

I hate that I know that feeling. I hate even more that I empathize with it. He sounds like he's the last person living in the entire world and he only just realized it. I felt that when my mother never came home and I realized I was the last Jaeger left.

For so much my life, my family was the compass I guided my actions by, whether I followed in their footsteps or to fight against harmful traditions. Being the last one means I am unmoored in a way that I still haven't quite wrapped my mind around.

I guess I'll figure that out when I get back to my realm. For now, I have answers to seek.

I slip fully back into my room and carefully close the shutters. Climbing down the exterior wall might work in a pinch, but it's a route I would like to avoid. There has to be a better way out of here that doesn't require wings.

But first I have to deal with dinner.

And the fact that this castle is freezing. The gargoyles may look human enough, at least at first glance, but their differences become more apparent as the minutes tick by. Obviously the same skin that protects them from the icy temperatures at higher altitudes also insulates them in everyday life. There's not even a fireplace in my room. I shiver and rub my hands over my bare arms, knowing full well that it won't do anything to actually warm me up.

He said something about clothing . . .

I move to the faded wardrobe tucked back in a corner. I half expect dust to explode in my face as I muscle it open, but it seems like it's been cleaned relatively recently. Inside, there are dozens of articles of clothing in a variety of styles. The one thing they all have in common is that they're about the same size and obviously made for colder climates. I shoot a glance at the door and quickly drag off my dress. It's tempting to go for the pants and long tunic, but I don't want to raise Bram's suspicions by making him think I want freedom of movement to fight or escape.

Instead, I pull on a thick dress that's almost exactly my size. The square neckline leaves most of my chest bare, but at least the dress has got long sleeves and plenty of layers to keep me warm. It's also about two inches too short, but I'm used to that. In the bottom drawer, I find woolen thigh-highs and ties to keep them up. That's enough to make me raise my brows. I don't know if Bram is allergic to clothing, but all he wore was a fancy-looking loincloth. There are no slits in the back of this dress to accommodate wings, so it was obviously created with a human in mind. The fact that there isn't a single undergarment to be found . . . I'm not sure what to think about that.

No, that's a lie. I know *exactly* what to think about that. I doubt whoever these clothes belonged to needed underwear. I read the contract Azazel gave me. I know that the opportunity for seduction is part of this. I even imagine that some people who make demon deals find fucking monsters to be a joy rather than a trial to avoid.

I can even admit that Bram himself is attractive. The wings are a bit overwhelming, and his skin doesn't feel like a human's, but it's not unpleasant either. There's a part of me that . . . No. I'm not going down that route. The only reason I'm here is to find answers about my mother, and I won't discover those by bouncing on a gargoyle's cock.

Though I have to play the game if I want him to let down his guard. That means allowing him to believe he has hope tonight so he won't watch me too closely when it's all said and done. By tomorrow, I'll be gone.

Again, a little twinge goes through me at the thought of honoring the word but not the spirit of Azazel's agreement. I promised seven years of service, and maybe I'm being unforgivable for essentially going back on my word, but I've done worse for poorer reasons.

In the bathroom, I find a brush and do my best to tame my wind-tangled hair. I don't bother with any of the cosmetics. There's also a sunken tub that was obviously designed for someone with wings because it's massive and shaped a little strangely. *Maybe if dinner is over quickly enough, I'll have time to soak for a while.*

No, that's an indulgence I can't afford. If I do anything to slow or stop my momentum, I might not get started again. I am . . . so tired. I shake my head shortly. "No use thinking about that. One step in front of the other, just like always."

To do exactly that, I walk out of the room and start down the hallway. I doubt it's time for dinner, with Bram out flying and venting his emotions to anyone who can see, but surely I'll run into someone who can point me to where dinner will be served.

And I'll get a look at the castle in the process.

Part of me thought that Bram dumped me in a mostly unoccupied wing of the castle and that was the reason there was no art on the walls or furnishings to be seen. There's not even a rug to warm the freezing stones beneath my stockinged feet. But apparently gargoyles don't believe in interior decorating at all. Every hallway and staircase is almost uniformly plain. If the gargoyles' goal is to ensure newcomers are hopelessly lost in minutes, they're doing a damned good job of it.

I make an effort to remember what turns I've made so I can find my way back to the room again, even if I have no intention of staying there for long. It's more difficult than I anticipated.

The other thing I notice is that the hallways are a lot larger than I expected, and I imagine a careful gargoyle could fly down them. Unfortunately, I don't have wings. The staircases give my poor human self vertigo, even though heights don't normally bother me.

In a place this big, there should be at least a small army of staff if not a shit-ton of other people wandering around. I won't pretend to be an expert on the demon realm and the politics of individual territories, but even in the brief moments I was outside of my room in Azazel's castle, I encountered a number of people.

This place feels deserted . . . Haunted, even.

There's a study several floors down from my room with a giant map pinned to the wall. I peer at it for several long moments. I can't read the text, but I'm pretty sure the mountains near the bottom are the ones we flew over to get here. We're not near the ocean, or at least I couldn't see it from the roof of this castle. There *was*, however, a lake. Just like the one on the map.

The only time I see another being is when I round a corner and almost stumble over a trio of young gargoyles. I'm still deciding if I'm supposed to smile or interact at all when they screech and flap their wings to put as much distance between us as possible. It startles me enough that I have to plant my feet to prevent backpedaling, which only makes them screech more. In seconds, they're gone, but it takes several beats longer for the sound of them to fade.

What the fuck was that?

I still don't have an answer an hour later when I finally find a door to the outside. I push through it, half expecting someone to appear and stop me, but the exterior is just as deserted as the interior. I inhale the cold air and do my best to smother my curiosity. It doesn't matter that this place is nothing like I expected. It doesn't matter that Bram seems to wear his sorrow the way some people wear clothes. All that matters is that there's no one around to stop me from leaving later tonight.

I study the area. There it is. The lake, just like the one on the map. It stretches to the north almost as far as the eye can see, ending in what appears to be a mountain ridge. Thankfully, I don't intend to head in that direction. It's pretty, though.

A bare whisper of sound announces Bram's arrival. He alights next to me almost delicately. I can't help searching his face for some sign of the anguish I witnessed, but he's got his expression locked down. His emotions aren't quite as controlled. White, pale blue, gray. This man is filled with grief and sorrow and worry. Somehow, I think it has nothing to do with me. It's certainly none of my business.

"Who did you lose?" I don't mean to ask the question. It's like my brain decided one thing and my mouth did the exact opposite.

He narrows those eerie pale-violet eyes at me. No, not violet. Lilac? I honestly don't know why I'm obsessing over the proper name for his eye color. The way he's watching me, it's almost as if he knows. But when he speaks, it's to answer my inappropriate question. "Everyone. I lost everyone."

I don't want to feel kinship with this man, but I can't help the answering ache that goes through me. "I see."

"Dinner should be ready soon enough." He pauses almost awkwardly. "You look really nice."

I can't help myself. I burst out laughing. "I'm wearing castoffs from someone else, I still have windburn all over my face, and I probably need a shower."

He moves quicker than he has right to, pressing one hand to the center of my back and leaning down, then dragging his nose along the line of my neck. It happens so fast, I can't figure out how I want to respond before he steps back and out of range again. "You smell good. Like the mountains. This way."

I stare after him for several seconds before I realize he means for me to follow. He just . . . sniffed me. I didn't hate it as much as I should have. In fact, my skin still tingles a little. It's an effort not to lift my hand and press my fingertips there, as if I can steal the sensation of his face against my skin.

I've had plenty of bed partners and even a scattering of relationships over the years. Not a single one of them was able to provoke a reaction on this level by doing so little. I want to blame his rugged attractiveness, but I am terrified that the real reason is because I can't help looking at him and suspecting that we are the same.

I've lost everyone too.

It's a good thing I'm getting the fuck out of here. My instincts are all messed up. If I spend any length of time with Bram, I might just fall right into his bed.

6

BRAM

I'm pleasantly surprised to find that dinner is delicious. Apparently my new cook knows what he's about, which is a relief. I'm not in a position to replace him. If he were terrible at his job, I'd just have to muscle through eating bad food in addition to everything else.

I find that I am a little embarrassed to seat Grace at this table with only the two of us. There are plates and chairs enough for twelve, but they sit empty tonight just like they always do. Most of the time, I eat by myself. I would love to do away with the damned table and the tradition that demands I take my place at the head of it every single night, but there's always the risk that one of the nobles in residence will attend. If they do, it's required that I have a place for them.

Grace watches me fill her plate and then mine, her curiosity a light green that covers the air. "Are we going to wait for everyone else?"

"There is no one else." I'm being too abrupt, my raw emotions making an ass of me. I'm supposed to be seducing this woman, not snapping at her over every innocent question. I take a deep breath and try again. "I'm the last of my family. It's tradition for the ruler of this territory to maintain a place at their table for each of the noble families. Sometimes they choose to attend, and sometimes they don't." No point in explaining that none of the families have chosen to attend dinner in years.

Grace picks up her fork and pokes at her food. "I'm the last of my family, too."

"I'm sorry." I make a face. "I don't know why I said that. They're pointless words that do absolutely nothing. And then it puts you in a position where you're supposed to say something back, and . . . what are you even supposed say to that? I never know."

Her lips curve in the first true smile she's given me. She was beautiful before, but with her dark-gray eyes lighting up, she's devastating. "Grief is a strange thing, isn't it?"

"The strangest." Especially in my case, when the cause for it wasn't something as simple and horrific as an accident or sickness. It wasn't chance that brought ruin upon my family. It was foolishness . . . and malice. But I know better than to say as much in dinner conversation with a person I'm attracted to. "I suppose it's taboo to ask about why you made a deal with Azazel."

"I am not entirely certain what is or isn't taboo with our current situation." She shrugs. "Several decades ago, a vampire saved my grandfather's life, and we incurred a life debt as a result. The old bastard couldn't stand to owe people, even someone he considered a monster. The rest of family took that sort of thing seriously. My grandfather was never asked to repay that debt, and neither was my father. So it fell to me. It gets a little complicated, but the short and simple version is that I agreed to pay the price of Azazel's bargain in order to balance the debt."

Fascinating. It's clear she's leaving a great swath of information out, but that makes sense since we just met. I'm curious about what her family does that put them in contact with vampires. We don't have vampires in this realm, but I was under the impression that they kept to themselves and away from humans. Or at least that's what our lore says, though it's severely out-of-date. "What will you do when the debt is paid and you go back?"

Her smile falls away. "I don't know. I'll probably follow up with Mina and her men and make sure they're okay. I feel a little guilty that I wasn't there to help more with her problems. She seemed like a good person."

Curiosity is a live thing inside me. "Do you help a lot of good people?"

"I don't know. I'd like to think I do, but some people might not feel the same way." She shakes her head. "But I guess after I check on her, I'll go back to what I was doing before. I haven't really thought about it." She takes a bite and chews. I'm still trying to decide if I should pursue the subject or try for something safer when she says, "What about you? Why did you agree to this deal? It seems pretty damned risky with very little reward."

She's not wrong. I debate whether to skirt the truth, but she'll figure it out before too long. I don't have to lay all my cards on the table to make her aware of the situation she's walked into. "I'm the last one in my family. This territory is essentially a monarchy, and I have no children to inherit. Because of . . . complications . . . none of the noble families are interested in marrying one of their own to me. If I die without an heir, they're contentious enough to devolve into a civil war, which will hurt all my people." I could leave it at that, but that would just feel dishonest. "There's an added factor in place as well, which is why all the territory leaders were invited by Azazel. Because of some quirk in the makeup of this realm, the strength of the magic of each territory is directly related to the strength of the magic of each territory leader. Everyone's magic has been fading for generations, ever since the realms split and crossing over became significantly more difficult."

Grace nods slowly. "Because humans are one hell of a conduit for your magic."

Again, she proves that she's no stranger to magical elements. Again, my distrust of her grows. "Only when it comes to breeding with them." I shrug, feigning nonchalance. "Any of the territory leaders who are able to convince their humans to procreate with them will have an edge over the others. It wasn't long ago that we were at war, and it's very present on everyone's mind that if war comes again, a half-human leader might mean the difference between victory and defeat."

She eats slowly, obviously mulling over the information I just imparted. Finally, she takes a sip of wine and sits back. "By the contract terms, you can't compel me to sleep with you. And you certainly can't force me to bear your child."

"I have no intention of forcing you to do anything. That's monstrous." Once again, the words come out too harsh. I know I should be focused on setting her at ease, but there are too many things *wrong*. Her comment about whether I burn. Her knowledge about the paranormal world. And that damned clause in Azazel's contract with me.

"Not to mention that you're not *able* to force anything." She takes another sip of wine. "If you harm me, your territory is forfeit."

I wonder if her low opinion extends to all people she considers monstrous or simply everyone who isn't her. "The contract is beside the point. You will not be forced."

"Then you're playing a losing game." She sighs. "If I'm stuck here for seven years, I don't want to be in a contentious relationship with you. It sounds exhausting for both of us, and I don't think you want that any more than I do."

She's not being honest with me. And she's not exactly lying, but her emotions are more muted than they have been since I met her, which means she's working hard to control them. It's not from fear. Out of all the emotions, fear is the one most challenging to mask. It's too instinctive.

"I agree," I say slowly. "You found your way down here well enough. Were you exploring?" I already know the answer, and I'm not certain if I'd rather her have cowered in her room until I came to retrieve her or not. I don't want her to fear me, but there's something dangerous about this woman. If she's a threat . . .

What will I do if she is? Run.

I take a large drink of wine. "Be careful on the stairs. A fall from a high floor will kill you."

"As I said before, I'm not afraid of heights and I've got excellent balance. I'll be fine."

"Right. Good." I sit back and swirl my wine in my glass. It's tempting to tell her that I doubt her intentions, but I can't help doubting *my* instincts. I'll be the first to admit that my opinions of humans are shaded by past events. It could be that I'm looking for trouble where there is none.

It could be, but I don't think so. I highly doubt Grace is here with good intentions. I won't know for sure until she acts, but I can keep a close eye on her.

I force a smile and allow her to believe the lie that I trust her. "I know this isn't easy for you. It isn't easy for me, either. There's plenty of time, Grace. We'll get to know each other slowly." It's a lie. There's a clock ticking down in my head. I don't believe the curse is real. That's nonsense. But enough bad things have happened that it's hard not to feel that I'm next. I won't breathe well until the line of succession is secured. Maybe not even then.

Dinner wraps up quickly after that. I escort Grace back to her room, and I don't miss the way she seems to be memorizing the trip. It's almost a relief that the hallways are empty and echoing—at least there's no one there to witness the growing awkwardness between us. I want to believe her memorization is so she can find her way through the halls while she lives here, but there's a quiet intent to her energy that speaks of slyness. It worms away from me every time I try to focus on it.

"Good night, Grace. I'll see you in the morning."

"Yes. See you in the morning." Guilt colors her emotions, and she shoots a quick look out the window. Looking for an escape route?

There's no violence in her right now, which leads me to only one possible conclusion. She's not here to attack anyone. She also has no intention of honoring her part of the bargain.

No, that can't be right.

Azazel gave her a chance to back out earlier. She didn't take him up on it. Why would she agree to this if she planned on fleeing the first chance she got?

Because I'm less of an obstacle than the bargainer demon.

Shame coats me, so thick I can barely breathe past it. I'm used to not being enough for my people, more or less, but this damned human doesn't know me.

She signed the contract, same as I did. She gave her word, same as I did. And yet she's not even going to wait twenty-four hours before she breaks it. I have no intention of forcing her into anything. I was going to give her the benefit of the doubt and conduct a slow seduction. I intended to get to know her and potentially craft a real relationship.

She had dinner with me to *placate* me. To make me think that we had a potentially real connection.

She lied.

As I ascend to the roof and crouch there, waiting for her to make her move, resolve solidifies inside me. If she doesn't intend to keep her word, then I won't either. I won't force her. I didn't lie when I said I have no desire or intention to do so.

But there is a lot of ground between a sweet seduction and force. It makes me a little sick to think of, but even that feeling falls away as full darkness descends and I catch the movement of Grace slipping out of the castle below.

She really thinks so little of me that she didn't even attempt to cover up her escape. There was no waiting for the deepest night to fall. She's not even moving particularly sneakily.

Anger blooms inside me, and I welcome it with open arms. It's so much easier to be angry than to drown in the damned shame that never leaves.

I take to the sky, using the cover of clouds to hide my movement. No matter how capable she is, she's on unfamiliar territory in the dark. There are many dangers in the lands around the castle, and I might be so furious I can barely breathe, but that doesn't mean I want her harmed.

She's prey and doesn't even know it.

She slips past the guard post with its spells that keep the area safe. I descend until I'm almost skimming the treetops, following the gray of her worry as she picks her way through the forest. Barely ten minutes have passed before a muffled curse sounds. Exactly as I expected. I find a spot and drop to the ground in front of her.

Grace hangs aloft, her entire body stuck to a massive web. She's taken the time to change out of her dress into a pair of leggings and a long tunic that puts her lean body on full display. She curses harder when she sees me, struggles more violently. All it does is entangle her further.

Overhead, something scurries along the web.

"The more you fight the web, the greater their frenzy when they reach you." I'm so angry, I hardly sound like myself. I approached this deal in good faith; Grace never intended to uphold her side of things.

"Cut me down, you bastard!"

I spread my arms. "I'll make you a bargain of my own, Grace." I don't wait for her to respond before I continue. "I don't know why you're so determined to flee, and I don't really care at this point. But if you're going to break your word, then so will I."

"What are you talking about?"

Now is the time to turn back, to not allow my anger to drive this situation. It's too late, though. I'm running out of time. More than that, I can't help looking at her and seeing the past play out in real time. Like my father, I went against the will of my people and brought a human into my home to be a potential partner. Like that human, Grace has gone back on her word and betrayed me.

Like that younger version of me, I wasn't good enough to stop it.

That should be reason enough to turn away from this course of action, but maybe I'm more similar to my monster of a father than I thought. Because I don't turn away. "You obviously want to run. I'll even let you. But every time I catch you, you will come to my bed willingly."

"Hard to call the sex willing if it's coercion," she snarls.

"Hard to call it honesty when all you do is lie."

The rustling overhead gets louder, closer. I don't look away from Grace as I strike out with my wings, using the spur to kill the spider stalking her. She doesn't scream when it drops and curls up on the ground below her feet, but her eyes get wide and her movements grow more frantic.

"I suggest you answer quickly. When they die, they give off a pheromone that draws others. They are not a wasteful species."

Grace looks up, and every bit of color leaches from her skin. Her energy surges with the light gray of fear. It's almost enough for me to back down. I hate this, but not enough to turn back. I had every intention of doing things with her the proper way, but she's taken that option from me with her betrayal.

Now only cruelty will do.

7

GRACE

I don't know who this man is, but he's not the nice, even awkward, gargoyle I shared dinner with. Bram stands in the shadows of the surrounding trees, his wings flared like a creature from a nightmare. I have to agree to his terms. The web is too sticky to escape from, and if the giant spider he killed is any indication . . . No, I can't think about the spider. I hate them in their small form in the human realm. I can barely comprehend the scale of the thing at my feet. It's got to be the size of a medium dog.

No, no, no, no, do not want, oh my gods, get me out of here.

There's a scream building in the back of my throat, a traitor of a sound, and if it escapes, I don't know if it'll ever stop. What happens when you spend twenty-five years not showing a single ounce of fear and then it all comes rushing out in a single instance? I'm terrified that I'll find out if Bram doesn't get me out of here right this fucking second.

"No babies." I don't have a single bit of bargaining power, and I know it, but I refuse to cross this particular line. Maybe I'm giving in too easily . . . or maybe him turning the bedroom into a battlefield is all too familiar. It's what I do, after all. Forcing this decision might be exactly what I need as an excuse to take what I want. It doesn't matter. There there's no way in hell I'm leaving a child behind in the demon realm.

"We'll see."

I ignore that. There's no time to bargain, no leverage to use to get what I want. "Every time I try to escape, if you catch me, I will come to your bed." I force myself to hold his gaze, or try to. His face is bathed in shadows. "But I'm not having your child."

"For now."

Something akin to pure heat flares inside me. This man is standing between me and the answers. The web is starting to vibrate with the movement of predators from above. I can't make myself look up. If I do, the scream I'm currently battling will win the war.

"I already agreed. Cut me down."

"Starting tonight." There is no give in his rough voice. I don't know if he really will stand here and watch me be eaten alive by giant spiders, but he looks pissed off enough to do it.

"Starting tonight." I yank on my arm, but all it does is make my entire body shake as my movement transfers to the web. Motion at the edge of my vision makes my head whip around despite my best efforts. I can't stop the whimper that slips from my lips. I would happily rather battle a rampaging minotaur with my bare hands than face what's skittering toward me on the web. "Bram, please!"

Once again, he strikes so quickly that I barely see the movement. This time, it's me that he cuts down. I barely have a second to attempt to brace myself before he catches me in his arms and launches us into the air. It's not cowardice that makes me cling to him, it's self-preservation. He might actually drop me.

He wings his way back to the castle and dives into one of the vertical shafts, using a speed that makes me breathless. Apparently we're not taking the slow way this time. It's hard to tell when everything looks exactly the same and I'm covered in web, but I think he takes me to a different part of the castle than my room is in. He lands with a grace that irritates me, and then he stalks to a massive double door at the end of the hallway. Inside is a room twice the size of mine and appointed just as luxuriously.

I tense, but he bypasses the bed without hesitation. Instead, he carries me into the bathroom and uses one of his wings to turn on the taps. He stands there in pained silence as water fills the tub. I open my mouth, but he silences me with a severe look. "I highly suggest you don't argue with me right now."

He's furious. It's written all over his aura, the starbursts of violent red. He might look like he hates me with his expression, but at least the sickly yellow-green-brown color is nowhere in evidence. I'm not about to examine why that absence fills me with relief.

For all Bram's anger, he holds me carefully. It would've been very easy for him to crush me or hurt me in some way, but even when we were flying furiously, he kept his arms in a comfortable bracket. It's more control than I would've been able to exhibit in his situation. I don't know if I find that to be a relief... or even more terrifying.

When the water is two-thirds full, he flips off the taps and sets me on my feet. I barely have a chance to reach for the hem of my shirt when he lightly smacks my hand out of the way.

And then the bastard cuts me out of my clothes with the wicked-looking spurs at the bending points of his wings.

It happens so fast, I'm still trying to process the fact that it's happening at all when I'm standing there before him. Naked. Did I really think I could control this man? That he wouldn't notice or care if I left?

I have made a terrible mistake.

I expect him to fall on me like a ravening beast, but he simply stands there and stares. It's almost worse. I can't remember the last time I felt this vulnerable. It takes everything I have to keep my hands at my sides and not try to cover myself—it would be ineffectual and would convey my fear all too clearly.

Finally, Bram stirs to life. With the flick of his wrist, his loincloth falls to the ground, and then he's just as naked as I am. Now it's my turn to stare. I knew he was larger than me, and I admit that part of me wondered if he was in proportion everywhere, but seeing it without any covering is a different experience altogether. I'd tried to convince myself that the very clear outline I saw earlier was simple a trick of the fabric.

It wasn't. His cock is fucking *huge*. It's also so hard that it looks painful. There's something strange about the shape, but he turns and descends into the bath before I can identify what.

He takes up a position facing me, his wings sliding easily into the curves of the tub. "The web will dissolve in water. You're not getting into my bed covered in that shit."

His harsh words snap me out of the reverie I fell into when I saw his cock. "You're the one who wants me in your bed. Now you're going to be picky on how I get there?"

"Yes."

Another time, I might dig my heels in out of sheer spite.

But the truth is that I want the webs off my skin and out of my hair just as much as he does. *More.* As long as I don't move, I can almost pretend they're not there. But every time I shiver, the stickiness makes my stomach twist into knots.

Even though the tub is deep, there aren't any stairs. It's downright awkward to step into it, and Bram doesn't offer to help. It's just as well. I would throw his help right back in his face.

Except . . . the water does feel good. I slip under the surface immediately and scrub my hands through my hair almost compulsively. By the time I rise back to the surface, the webs are all but gone. Thank fuck.

But without the webs to distract me, the reality of my situation slams home. I'm naked, in a bathtub with an equally naked Bram. For his part, he just sits there with that immovable look on his face that makes me want to throw myself against him until one of us shatters.

He knows I plan to leave again.

If he catches me, he'll bring me back again and fuck me.

I shiver at the thought, and I can't begin to say if it's fear or lust causing the physical reaction. If I could see my own aura, I wouldn't be able to lie to myself like that, so it's just as well that I can't. Bram might have me over a barrel with this bargain, but that doesn't mean I have to play the whimpering, terrified human to his monster. I'll make him regret ever having me in his bed as part of the terms.

I duck under the water again to ensure the last of the webs are gone. When I rise, it's to stand before him. The tub is deep enough that the water comes up to my waist, but that leaves my breasts on full display. He notices too. His attention fastens on my chest; he can't seem to make himself look away.

Something almost like power surges inside me. I

intended to stay out of this man's bed, but now that the choice is taken away from me, I feel a little free As if, for the first time in my life, I don't have to worry about being palatable to a lover. I can just be me. "You've made a mistake, and now I'm going to make you choke on it."

He lifts a single dark brow. "You're so quick with your words, and yet your actions never follow through. Do it."

I flush at the reminder that I broke my word. Oh well. We're here now, and I have no interest in making sure this train stays on the tracks. I cross to him before I can think of all the reasons I shouldn't, and it's like once I'm in motion, all my reservations fall away. I can tell myself I don't have a choice, but the truth is that he's not doing a single thing except sitting there, watching me with a challenge in his light eyes. He doesn't think I'll follow through on this. That, more than anything, spurs me on.

I drift my fingers over the surface of the water and lift my hands to cup my breasts. "Poor little gargoyle. Not a single one of your people will have you. Reduced to slumming it with a human."

"You said it. I didn't."

My flush deepens, and I tell myself it's the heat of the bath causing it and not the sting of his words. He doesn't stop me from moving forward, though. In fact, when my legs bump against his, he spreads his thighs to allow me closer. "A human who doesn't even want you. One you have to coerce into your bed."

If anything, his expression becomes more mocking. "Yes, Grace. You seem to be exceedingly coerced right now." Once again, his attention falls to where I cup my breasts and toy with my nipples. "Practically quivering with . . . fear."

I want to shut him up. That's the only thing I'm thinking when my body springs into motion. I straddle him and sink my hands into his long white hair before jerking his head back and exposing his throat. "I could kill you right now."

His eyes slide halfway shut, and an unexpected smile curves his lips. His wings move. I tense, expecting him to knock me back. Instead, he smacks a small table just behind him. I didn't even notice it was there. There's a flash of flying metal, and then his hand snaps out to catch a dagger. He did it all without moving his head from my grasp.

What the fuck?

Bram grabs my wrist and pulls my hand out of his hair. I'm shocked enough to let him do it. He presses the dagger hilt to my palm and guides it to his exposed throat. "You want to kill me? Then do it."

Shock stills me. I search his face, his aura, for proof this is a bluff. All I find is the deep violet of resolve threaded with the pale mauve of relief. He means it. I don't know what to make of this puzzle of a man. Maybe I should cut his throat and be done with it. Except that would break Azazel's contract. Time moves differently in this realm, and it's entirely possible that he hasn't yet fulfilled his part of the bargain to save Ryland and the others and deliver them to Mina. I tell myself that's the only reason I do what I do next —I can't afford to let that happen. I toss the dagger away.

I *save* people. I don't kill them.

I kiss Bram.

8

BRAM

There's no hesitation in Grace as she takes my mouth. A part of me whispers that I should be taking charge, but I'm so fucking tired. Tired of fighting a losing battle that never seems to end. Tired of the constant reminders of all the ways I don't measure up. Just . . . tired.

It feels good to have Grace's hands in my hair, pulling just hard enough to hurt. For her mouth to move against mine, nipping my bottom lip to tease my mouth open. She's tastes like nothing I've ever experienced.

Then she sinks into me, pressing her whole body against mine. She's such a little thing for someone so fierce. I could break her in half without even trying.

And yet I find myself sitting here passively while she dominates me with the single greatest kiss of my life. It's been years since I've been this close to another person, let alone . . .

Grace yanks on my hair again, harder this time. "Have you changed your mind?" There's a challenge in her tone, but she doesn't otherwise move while she waits for my answer.

Have I?

A naive, foolish part of me wanted something different with the opportunity Azazel offered. Something real. To prove that *I'm* not the curse in action. I should have known better. It was always going to end like this.

A vicious fight instead of a delicate seduction.

"Have you?" I bite out.

She rises enough to study my face. A cutting smile pulls at her lips. Her energy is an overwhelming mix of bright pink and red, lust and anger driving her the same way it's driving me. "No," Grace says slowly. She shakes her head as if coming out of a trance. "But no babies."

I might be able to provoke her into forgetting that rule, but part me still wants there to be some lines I don't cross. "I'll get you a birth control pendant tomorrow."

She blinks. "A birth control pendant. That sounds . . ." Another shake of her head. "We'll circle back to that."

"Sure." It's difficult to think with her breasts pressed against my chest. So I don't bother. I still can't get enough of Grace's fingers in my hair. I like it a lot. Especially when she wraps my hair around one fist and then moves her other hand up to trace a finger along one of my horns.

Her expression is still pure evil, but I find I don't mind at all. "You're getting your way, Bram. Me in your bed. You can't fuck me tonight, but other than that . . . what are you going to do to me?"

The question should feel almost vulnerable, but it comes out the same way everything does from Grace. Like a challenge.

I don't answer with words. Instead, I hook my hands under her ass and lift her mostly out of the water. She's not quite passive in my hold, not with that imperious look in her dark eyes, but she allows me to maneuver her. Likely because I've essentially made a seat for her with my hands. A throne, even. She certainly has the energy of a queen.

Now, finally, I can look at her to my heart's delight.

She's well-formed, my vicious human. Long and lean, with strong muscles that stand out as she shifts restlessly. And scars. I hadn't noticed before when she was wearing the purple dress, and she was more effectively covered with the other dress, but my Grace has scars all over her body. Some are faint and silvery and nearly entirely faded. Some are recent enough to be pink against her fair skin.

I trace a large one on her thigh with my thumb. "What happened here?"

"The same thing that happened everywhere else." She says it in a bored tone. Not even her energy shifts.

Again, I feel a kinship with this woman. I know that tone. I've used it myself many times when recounting what happened to my family. Sometimes it's easier to cut out emotions entirely than to deal with them every time a subject comes up.

I don't ask her again. Really, it doesn't matter. I didn't bargain for her history. I bargained for her in my bed. That will have to be enough.

She'll take control of this situation in a heartbeat. I can already see the calculation on her face as she shifts, her skin slick against my palms where I hold her aloft. There's a part of me that desperately wants to let her do it. The moment when she dug her fingers into my hair and held my knife to my throat . . .

I've never felt more at peace.

I crave a repeat experience more than I crave the feeling of the wind buoying me in the air. Which is why I can never let her know how much I want it. Grace is a predator through and through. She wants to leave, and if she thinks she can dominate her way into doing it, she won't hesitate. I'm not certain how I'd respond to such a thing, so I can't allow us to get there.

"Spread your thighs."

She tightens her grip, one hand still in my hair. "I thought you wanted me in your bed."

"Next time." If I have her in my bed now, I'm not certain we won't get carried away. Maybe that's a foolish thing to worry about when we've kissed a single time, but the energy between us is a biting, feral thing. It feels like we're a single action away from an explosion. I don't know what will be left if that happens.

I'll keep my word to her, even if she isn't interested in giving me the same courtesy.

"Spread your legs, Grace. Give me your pussy."

The pink in her energy creates a torrent around us so bright, I almost have to close my eyes. But I couldn't even if I wanted to, not when she holds me captive in her gaze. I'm incapable of doing anything but remaining still as she slowly spreads her thighs before hooking her feet on the outside of my shoulders.

Her pussy is as beautiful as she is. Pretty and pink and glistening with need.

"Do you want me to play your sick little game, Bram? Make it worth my while." She pulls on my hair again roughly. "Make me come so hard, I can't wait to get your hands and mouth on me again. Do it now, before I change my mind."

In another world and another life, I would try to slow us down and turn this sweet instead of harsh. But this isn't another world. It isn't another life. I only have the one, as fucked up as it is.

I hold Grace closer and obey exactly as she commands, exactly as I crave. I drag my tongue up her center. She tastes even better than she looks, and the little sound she makes is so at odds with the woman I'm starting to know, I can't help the compulsive need to make her do it again. If I can coax her to lose control, maybe I'll gain a little of it for myself.

I've never had sex with a human, though, and I'm achingly aware of our differences in size and strength. Grace feels larger than life as she guides my mouth to her clit, but the truth is, she's not. I could crush her all too easily. In a way, it's a relief that she's guiding this. All I have to do is make a shelf with my hands and follow her instructions.

"You're holding back." Her voice has gone strange and breathy, but that doesn't change the fact that my spine snaps straight at the criticism. I move her back just enough that I can see her face. Her brows are drawn together in consternation. "*Have* you changed your mind?"

I might laugh if I had the breath for it. Change my mind? It's everything I can do to hold perfectly still and only move my mouth and tongue. To go slow instead of devouring her the way I'm craving. To not haul her to my bed and see if her pussy takes my cock as sweetly as it takes my tongue. Reckless. I am so fucking reckless. "No," I manage. "I haven't changed my mind."

She's still watching me as if she doesn't quite believe me. "Maybe we should—"

"If you remember, *I'm* the one who brought you here for this purpose. I have not changed my mind, Grace." Need makes me too harsh, though that's a pathetic excuse for what I say next. "I'm easily twice your size, with claws, wings, and fangs. I could kill you half a dozen ways in seconds. Forgive the fuck out of me if I'm trying to ensure you stay safe and whole through this process." *Why the fuck did I say that?* I'm acting the part of exactly the monster she thinks I am. No good man reminds the people around him of all the ways he can hurt them, even if it's the truth. But then, I'm not a good man, am I? I forced her into the corner, and now I'm being a dick about it.

Grace doesn't demand I release her. She doesn't tell me to fuck off. She doesn't do anything but stare at me with that same strange look on her face that I keep seeing over and over. As if I'm a puzzle box she hasn't quite solved.

"You won't hurt me." She says it so confidently, I almost believe her.

I can't afford to. Explaining means admitting something that I would rather not, but I need her to understand the severity of the situation we find ourselves in. "I wouldn't intentionally hurt you. But it's been . . . quite some time for me. I might be able to afford to lose control with one of the people in this realm, but humans are significantly more fragile."

She smiles slowly, and my cock jerks in response. "You're making it very hard to hate you right now."

"Do you have to hate me?"

"Yes." She looks around and seems to focus on something behind me. "If you're that concerned with hurting me, I can just bind you until I'm done having my filthy way with you. How does that sound?"

It sounds like a terrible fucking idea. She's already proven she's not trustworthy, and making myself helpless in any true way is a mistake. She's just as likely to tie me up and then take off again. But, fool that I am, I find myself saying, "It sounds good."

I expect her to guide us into the bedroom. I really

should've known better. I end up sitting on the cool tile of the bathroom as she uses a piece of ripped-up sheet to tie my hands at the small of my back. She's clever about it too. She ensures that I have my wings trapped by my arms before she binds my wrists. It's a strange kind of compromise. I'm helpless in a way, but it will be easy enough to rip free of the bindings if I need to.

Then she pushes me onto my back.

I am a winged creature. There is no more unnatural position than lying on my back with my wings pinned. Every instinct demands that I roll, fight, do something to get free. Instead, I lie there as she sits on my chest. Grace sifts her fingers through my hair almost gently. "You're strong enough to topple me if you want me to stop, but if you prefer a different method of tapping out, I'm all ears."

Tapping out. The very idea is laughable. Her pussy is so close, and I can still taste her on my tongue. I would happily drown in her. "That's not necessary."

"And yet here I am, telling you that if you want to stop, all you need to do is sit up." She frowns at me. "*Can* you sit up with me right here?"

Instead of responding with words, I surge up and topple her into my lap. Far from being irritated by it, she gives another evil laugh, and then her hands are back in my hair. Grace kisses me as if she wants to take the very air from my lungs. Then she shoves me back down. "Good boy. You can also tap your foot on the ground. If you do that, we'll stop."

"I don't want to stop," I snarl.

"All the same." She brushes her thumb over my bottom lip. "Now I'm going to ride your face until I come. If you're very, very good and make me come very, very hard, once I'm satisfied, I'll suck that fancy cock of yours."

9

GRACE

There's no time for thinking, no time for second guesses. Not with my need riding me so hard and Bram's lust so thick in the air that I can taste it on my tongue. This man, this predator, might not be helpless, but he's on his back and tied down for me. Most of the time, when my need gets too strong and my willpower too weak, I sleep with other hunters. There's a strange comfort in the fact that they don't bother with small talk the way normal people do. The downside is that I am keenly aware of the power balance between me and my partners. When you're a hunter, letting your guard down means welcoming death. It means that even sex is another kind of battle.

It should feel like that with Bram. It *is* like that with Bram. He "rescued" me so that he could force me into his bed, but I don't feel forced at all. I feel . . . powerful.

I move back to straddle his face and prop my hands on the floor. The way he stares at my pussy borders on devoted. He actually licks his lips. If this man knows how to lie, I'll eat my shirt.

There's no point in another reminder that he knows how

to stop this. He's proven he does. Any more talking is me chickening out. There's nothing else to do but lower myself onto his mouth. I've always loved oral sex, but it's a relatively rare experience for me. Both giving and receiving. There's too much vulnerability in it, and having sex is vulnerable by nature, so I've rarely sought the deeper layers of it.

Bram goes after me with no hesitation. He kisses my pussy as if he'll never get enough, devoting attention to every single inch of me. He delves his tongue inside, and my eyes threaten to roll back in my head. He's big enough that I feel like he could swallow me whole.

It hits me all at once that I'm letting him guide this. That wasn't the plan. "My clit. Make me come."

He doesn't hesitate. He stops fucking me with his tongue and shifts so that he can rub the flat of it against my clit. I curse, or gasp, or whimper. I can't identify the sounds coming out of my mouth. It feels so fucking good to give myself over to pleasure without worrying about the rest. I have no choice, after all.

Except that's a lie.

He's not holding me down. He hasn't tied me up the way I've tied him up. He hasn't done more than some ham-handed coercion. If I had dug in my heels at any point, I have a feeling he would've folded.

It doesn't matter. I embrace the lie because there is freedom in it. I ride his mouth, grinding down on his tongue with an abandon I never would've shown with a past partner. Bram seems to love it, if his growls vibrating against my clit are any indication.

I can't stop. I am a mindless thing, devoted to my pleasure. I need to come. I think I might die if I don't.

It crests over me, the feeling that's been building and building, and yet the strength of it still catches me off guard.

I cry out. My thighs start to shake. And then I'm collapsing on Bram's face. Not that he seems to mind. He delves his tongue back inside me as if trying to lick up every drop of my orgasm. It sets off another, smaller, explosion, and I sob my way through that orgasm as well.

What did he do *to me?*

He gives me one last long lick and sits up slowly, toppling me into a boneless heap on his lap. I blink up at him, expecting arrogance or satisfaction, but there is no one at home in his pale eyes. He pants, his breath coming just as hard as mine. "More."

I want more too. If he can do that with both hands tied behind his back, what more can he do with his entire body in play? I desperately want to know the answer. But I can't find out tonight. It's too dangerous. I fight to clear my throat. "Give me a few seconds to recover, and I'll take care of you."

"I don't give a fuck about that, Grace." He bends his legs, lifting my body toward him again so he can drag his tongue over the curve my breast. "I'm not done with you. Untie me. Let me touch you."

If I let him touch me, I'm going to end up on his cock. I'll regret it in the morning, but the need will be too much to deny tonight. It will override what little common sense I have left. Even now, my mind is doing backflips to justify giving him exactly what he wants. What we both want.

I . . . can't do it.

"No," I finally manage. But I arch my back and give him better access to my nipple. He sucks me hard, drawing forth another whimper and an answering pulse in my pussy. Fuck, but I need him. I should be sated after that orgasm—two orgasms, really. Instead, my desire burns hotter.

I have to do something to get control of the situation, or I'm going to end up riding his cock. My body tightens at the thought. That's what gets me moving. I slide off his lap and shimmy backward into the bathtub. I'd like to pretend that I intentionally submerge myself, but the truth is that my body isn't quite working as well as I'd like it to. When I resurface, Bram is staring at me as if he wants to devour me whole.

I want that. I want that far too desperately.

Which is why I need to stay in the tub, and he needs to stay out of it.

I shift to the edge and wrap my hands around the back of his knees. "Come here." I couldn't move him if I wanted to, but he wastes no time scooting to the edge. I end up between his thick thighs with his outstanding cock at chest level. And it *is* outstanding. I got a glimpse of it before, but I wasn't sure if I was seeing things correctly. Turns out I was right. There are ridges along his length.

I skate my fingers over his thighs to his hips. "I'm going to suck your cock now. Be good and hold perfectly still. If you want me to stop, say stop." He's big. Really big. Big enough that there's a little scattering of fear through my lust. It heightens the sensation, but the truth is that I don't know if I can take him. Certainly not with abandon—not if I want to walk the next day. And if he lost control and fucked my mouth . . . Best not to let that happen.

I can't help touching him, though. I wrap my fist around his cock as much as I'm able to and pump slowly, letting myself imagine how those subtle ridges will feel inside me. Good. Better than good. I can't fucking wait. I reach the crown of his cock and squeeze. A drop of pre-come is my reward.

"Grace. Please." His voice is so rough, it sounds like someone is strangling him.

I like it when he begs. I've never really experimented with kink, though I'm more than passingly familiar thanks to the reading I've done on the subject. I never could've anticipated the thrill his submission gives me. I squeeze his cock again. "Please, what?"

He growls deeply enough that I swear I feel my bones vibrate. "If you don't stop doing that, I'm going to come before you even get your mouth on me."

I both want that and don't want that. There's a part of me that desires drawing this out until we're both too exhausted to go on. An equally strong part wants to see if I can actually make him come just from teasing. The fact that I affect him just as deeply as he affects me is a comfort.

I hold his gaze as I lean down and lick the pre-come from his slit. His eyes slide shut, and another growl emerges from his lips. I want to hear—no, feel—him make that sound when he's inside me. But not tonight.

"You made me come so hard." I lick his cock again. "It's making me feel particularly generous. So I'll give you a choice."

"What choice?"

"I'll let you choose where you come." His eyes fly open in shock, and I have to muscle down my smile. "My lips." I drift them over his cock. "My throat." I guide his cock to my throat and drag it down the center. "Or my breasts." I rise out of the water enough to rub his cock along first one nipple and then the other.

Bram is breathing so hard, his chest heaves with every inhale. The veins stand out on his arms, and I honestly can't tell if he's trying to break free of his bindings or fighting against the urge to snap them. Each exhale carries more rough growls. "You're a menace, woman."

"Only mostly." I don't stop rubbing his cock over my breasts. It's such a light touch, and yet I can feel my heartbeat in my nipples and pussy. I'm playing a dangerous game. We both are. "Choose."

"I—" He tenses. "Suck my cock and then make me come all over your tits. I want to mark you, however temporarily."

It scares me how much I want that too. He barely finishes speaking when I descend to take his cock into my mouth. Really, he *is* too big. I can't suck him properly. It doesn't matter. Not when his thighs go rigid on either side of me and his growls get deeper and longer. I suck and lick at him, letting my hands do most of the work. It feels almost like desperation. I *need* him to lose control the same way I did. I need him to mark me the same way my desire still marks his face.

"Grace."

I don't require any further warning. I pull back and use both hands to jack him, pointing his cock at my chest. He lets out a sound that's part curse and part my name. And then he comes all over my chest. An impossible amount. It just keeps going, him lashing me with spurt after spurt until my breasts are all but covered.

I've never felt more powerful in my life. I release his cock and drag my finger through his seed. "Look at the mess you made."

"*Grace.*" There's a warning in his voice, and I look up at his face, startled. That's when I realize he snapped the bindings and his hands are free. He places his hands very carefully on his thighs. His gaze is fastened to my breasts as if he can't make himself look away. "Let me make you come again. Please. You have my word that I won't give my cock to your needy pussy, even if you beg for it."

That way lies danger.

I want what he's offering. Gods, I want it. But if I climb out of this tub and into his lap, I will end up begging him for his cock. I can't guarantee any promises we make right now will hold if that happens. So I do one of the hardest things I've ever done in my life.

I take a step back.

Bram shakes his head slowly as if coming out of a dream. "Very well." It takes him two tries to find his feet. Another time, I might find that incredibly satisfying, but I'm too focused on keeping my mouth closed—so I don't call him back—to appreciate how thoroughly I have ruined him. He leaves the bathroom several seconds later, and it's another few beats before I hear the bedroom door close and know that I'm alone.

Only then do I sink beneath the surface and scream out my frustration.

That was too close. On multiple counts.

10

GRACE

I'm not sure where it all went pear-shaped.

I lie on my bed and stare up into the vaulted ceiling, my body still singing from Bram's mouth. My *soul* still singing from the way he yielded. I've never considered myself particularly kinky, or at least not in the way that requires elaborate rules and playacting scenes. But what happened in the bath . . . The power that coursed through me when he followed my demands. The surrender in his pale eyes. It's just as heady as his tongue on my clit.

A problem. That's what this is. Nothing more than a problem. I must have done something to arouse his suspicions at dinner. Leaving on the first night was too impulsive. Of course he's going to keep an eye on his investment. Just because this castle seems deserted doesn't mean it's actually empty.

I . . . did not expect that from Bram, though. Not the anger and not the ruthlessness. Even now, I'm not entirely certain he wouldn't have left me to the spiders if I hadn't agreed. There was no mercy on his brutal face when he laid out the terms.

If I run and he catches me, he'll drag me back to his bed.

I shiver and flop onto my stomach. The change in the gargoyle should scare me. It makes him a threat in a way he wasn't previously. I know what my mother's advice would be —eliminate the threat before it can eliminate me—but for some reason my brain won't quite make the leap with me.

He hasn't hurt anyone to my knowledge. He certainly hasn't hurt me. I might be barred from bargainer demon territory, but that's at least partially my fault. Bram isn't actually a monster, and I only kill monsters.

He would have let me slit his throat in the tub. There was no hesitation in his aura, no trap waiting to be sprung. Bram is . . . complicated.

I don't have time for complicated right now. Not when I'm so close to the answers I've sought for years. If there's a part of me that unfurls at the challenge . . . Well, I've always had a bit of a self-destructive streak. It's kind of hard to be a monster hunter without one. We don't die of old age.

I roll onto my back again, restless. I have to run again. Giving up after one attempt is out of the question. I'll just be more careful next time, sneakier. Now that I know the forest is filled with *that* kind of threat, I can be more prepared. The trees should inhibit Bram from getting to me from the air.

Even if they didn't inhibit him from finding me in seconds after I got snared by that web.

"No. Damn it, *no*. I can do this."

I'm still examining the problem from various angles when sleep sneaks in and takes me.

I awake some time later to the sound of movement in my room. I don't open my eyes, change my breathing, or otherwise stir, but a second later a vaguely familiar voice filled with amusement says, "I know you're awake. You're practically seething with anger that I'm in your space. It's rather delicious."

I open my eyes and sit up. I expected a gargoyle, but this person isn't one. They're a bargainer demon, though they're nowhere near the size of Azazel. They're also missing their eyes, a second set of dark horns sprouting from their eye sockets. The same demon who gave me the translation tattoo. It takes a second to place their name: Ramanu. "I thought you weren't supposed to check in for days yet."

"Mmm, that's true enough." They lift a candle from the dresser, appear to examine it, and set it down with a careless grace. They're wearing a black garment that might be a jumper or a dress, but I can't quite make heads or tails of it. "At least for the others. But you're special, aren't you, Grace?"

I narrow my eyes, searching their aura for some indication of what they're up to. There's nothing but a deep-yellow amusement and a hint of light-green curiosity. "Special is one way of putting it."

"You make it sound like I'm insulting you." They clutch their chest, though their amusement never falters. "But we both know you're not insulted. You're curious." They move closer, though they stay well out of striking range. "Just like you know I'm amused right now. A deep yellow in my energy, yes?"

I flinch. Of all the things I expected them to say, that didn't number among the options. "What are you talking about?"

"No point in lying. Again, something you should know just by looking at me. *I'm* not lying." They grin, flashing teeth in a way that feels both threatening and like they're laughing at me. Their words seem to suggest they know about my ability, but that's impossible. As if sensing my disbelief, they chuckle. "Come now, little hunter. I know what your family is. Surely they're more aware than most of the histories. One of my parents is a gargoyle, which is what gave me my good looks." They motion at their face. "And my ability to read emotions and magic. Just like one of *your* ancestors indulged with a gargoyle, and that ability has likely been skipping down your family line ever since."

There's no lie in their aura. They genuinely believe what they're saying. I shake my head, my mind reeling. "That's impossible." Oh, not that one of my ancestors strayed to a paranormal partner and had a child—that's the only way humans can get any magic of their own. But a gargoyle? That means . . . I freeze. "All gargoyles have this ability?"

"Mm-hmm." Their grin goes a little mean. "You look well sated, so whatever you've done to piss Bram off isn't unforgivable. However, it would be wise to remember that he can read you exactly as thoroughly as you can read him."

I press my hand to my mouth. If that's true . . . No wonder he didn't believe me. He could read the lies right in my aura. "Damn." That complicates things. In all my travels and years monster hunting, I've never met another being outside my family who could do what I do. Until now.

Because they've all been in the demon realm.

"Now that we've established I can call you on your bullshit, let's talk." They drop onto my bed in a motion that's nearly a flounce. "Azazel is concerned you're going to go on a murderous rampage and endanger all the plans he's spent so long curating. I also happen to have a vested interest in the peace he's seeking, which means I am equally concerned. I know he gave you a chance to back out of this particular part of the contract. I'm extending that offer a second time."

I stare. "Somehow, I don't think Azazel would appreciate you speaking so frankly."

"Probably not." They wave that away breezily. "But he's not here. It's just us." They roll onto their side, facing me, and prop their head up in one hand. The second set of horns really is a bit disconcerting, mostly because I feel like they're studying me. Probably because they are. I don't need my eyes open to read auras if I concentrate. Ramanu doesn't need eyes at all to do the same.

I don't move away though they're entirely too close for comfort. "I have no intention of murdering anyone." At least not until I find out what happened to my mother, and only then if there's someone specifically responsible for her death.

"That's a rather large caveat you're not saying." They snort. "Listen, I like you, so—"

"You don't even know me. We've been talking for less than five minutes."

They ignore my interruption. "I notice you're not jumping at the chance to return to bargainer demon territory. I wonder why that is."

They're right. I should have agreed the second they offered, just like I should have taken Azazel up on *his* offer. "If I come back, is anyone going to tell me the truth about what happened?"

"Unlikely. Everyone has secrets, and I expect Azazel has a particular reason for keeping this one close to his chest."

That's what I thought. Still, my whole goal was to go back and find answers. I don't know why I'm hesitating. "Am I going to be locked up for the next seven years?"

Ramanu shrugs. "Who can say? That castle is so wily. It has a mind of its own."

I couldn't pick the lock in the three days I was there

before the auction. That doesn't bode well for me being able to do it in the future. If I accept Ramanu's offer, then I'll be stepping into an even more complicated cell. At least here, I have free range and a chance to escape.

The logic feels flimsy at best, but I ignore it.

"No, thanks."

"Thought you might say that." Their grin is a little mean. They flick their fingers and a ring appears between their claws. "Take this. If you change your mind, hold it and say my name and I'll come."

"Ramanu."

We both jump as Bram climbs in through my window. I have nothing to feel guilty for, but I can't help scooting away from Ramanu. Those few extra inches between us don't feel like much with Bram glowering down at us. He's halfway across the room, but it doesn't seem to make a difference. I'm not *scared* of him, but I'm not a fool; of course I'm wary.

Ramanu, on the other hand, seems unconcerned that Bram is looking at their throat like he wants to rip it out with his teeth. They reach over and twine a lock of my hair around their claws. Bram is so focused on that hand, he doesn't see them slip the ring into my other. "I came to check in on the well-being of Azazel's human."

"She's not *his*."

I don't understand Bram. There are times when it feels like I can almost read his thoughts, when I feel a connection deeper than skin and bone, but then he turns around and does something to act against the little box I instinctively put him into. The man glowering at us is not the same man who offered me his throat without reservation. He's dangerous.

I start to sit up. "Bram—"

"It's fine." Ramanu releases me and rises with a fluid

grace that sets alarm bells pealing through my head. "Bram may be reckless, but he's not a fool. To lay a finger on me is to directly challenge Azazel. He can't afford to do that because he won't win."

The comment should fill me with relief, but all I feel is anger at the defeat that flickers over Bram's expression. I might not know which way is up and which way is down in this current situation, but I know a shit-starter when I see one. Ramanu might technically be here to check on me, but they're also here to stir the pot. That's the last thing I need. "I think you should go."

"Ah, but I haven't finished telling you everything you need to hear." They hold up two long crimson fingers tipped with black claws. "One. Bram didn't want to take the deal, but he had no choice. None of his people will have him. They believe he's cursed and that anyone who gets close to him will become victim to the curse." Bram makes a choked noise, but they ignore him. "Two. Azazel understands your motives for being here, but make no mistake—you are expected to hold to your end of the bargain. If you do so for the agreed upon time, he is prepared to tell you everything you want to know about your mother."

It's a low blow. Azazel knows exactly how desperately I want that information, so of course he's willing to hold it over my head to ensure good behavior. Unfortunately for him, I wouldn't know good behavior if it bit me in the ass.

Considering Ramanu offered to see me to the bargainer territory earlier, it's easy enough to read between the lines of *this* offer. If I go with them, there's a decent chance Azazel will never answer my questions. I grit my teeth. I *will* get answers. I'm so close, it makes me a little sick to my stomach.

Resolve solidifies inside me. I will stay here, and I will find my own way to answers. "I understand."

Their mouth quirks into a strange little smile. "Aren't you the entertaining little liar? This is going to be great fun."

Next to them, Bram is practically vibrating with fury. "Get. Out."

Far from being intimidated, Ramanu just laughs. "Darling, there's only one person I take orders from, and it's not you. It's cute that you try, though." They pat Bram on his shoulder and waltz out of the room with a little sway in their hips.

Through it all, they didn't technically do anything threatening or wrong, but that doesn't change the fact that I feel threatened. This might've been a check-in to ensure I was safe, but it's blatantly clear that Azazel doesn't trust me even though he also wants to protect me. Or something. The longer I think about this tangled web of bargains and promises, the less clear it seems. I'm missing something obvious and important.

Maybe he intends to honor the specific words of the bargain, but not the spirit of it. I'm sure there's some clever loophole I'm not seeing. Something like him telling me *what* happened, but not *why* it happened. Or, gods, what's to keep him from lying? His word? Don't make me laugh.

Azazel is playing as many games as Ramanu.

Bram is still glowering at me in a way that makes me fight a shiver. I can't even pretend it's fear, when I can still clearly feel the memory of his tongue inside me. That, more than anything, gets my mouth running before I can think better of it. "I'm surprised you didn't tell them what happened last night. They're already aware I'm a problem child. Maybe you could've switched me out for a more compliant human." I don't know why I say it. If I wanted to go back to the bargainer territory, I would have taken Ramanu up on their offer.

He moves to stand between me and the door "You're right. If they knew you were trying to escape, they would take you from me."

He's only echoing my own thoughts. It still feels like a slap in the face. "Yes, I believe that is exactly what I just said," I snap.

He doesn't move toward me, but the way he shifts his wings makes the room feel significantly smaller. "We discussed this last night, Grace. This is between you and me. You can try to escape to your heart's content. I will track you down and bring you back to my bed every single time." Without another word, he turns and walks out of my room, shutting the door softly behind him.

11

BRAM

I'm not remotely surprised to find Ramanu waiting for me at the bottom of the staircase. They lean against the wall, the very essence of unconcerned. It's a lie. I can see the threads of gray worry flickering through their energy. I've had enough interactions with them over the years to know they can hide their emotions when they feel the need, so they're intentionally letting me know. One of their parents is a distant cousin of mine, and that should be enough to create a bond between us, but Ramanu is too cunning to trust. They always seem to be playing games at a level beyond anyone else in the room.

It irks me.

"You haven't told her about what happened to your family."

Even expecting this conversational turn, I have to fight to keep from snarling. I don't have a problem with Ramanu normally, but finding them in Grace's bed has not endeared them to me in the least. "I told her what she needs to know."

They shake their head slowly. "I argued against this. You've got too much baggage when it comes to humans, and while Grace is hardly a normal human, the fact remains that she *is* in danger every moment she spends with you. You can read my emotions. I can read yours. Let's not dance around this. You're a danger to yourself, Bram, and if you're careless with yourself, you could hurt Grace."

They aren't wrong, but that doesn't mean I'll admit as much out loud. "I would never hurt Grace." I can't argue that I'm not a danger to myself, because I am. I can't even pretend I'm not a danger to others, because while I might never intend to hurt those around me, my cowardice ensures I'll never help them either.

"Maybe. Maybe not." All the playfulness is gone from their voice, leaving only a hard edge. "Azazel may have agreed to this bargain, but part of that agreement is regular check-ins with me to ensure Grace's well being. I don't know what the fuck happened with the two of you, but if she's still twisted up the next time I come, I will take serious consideration into removing her from your care. Regardless of whether or not she wants to leave."

Fury unlike I've ever known surges through me. "I respect you and what you're doing here, but if you attempt to remove Grace from my home, I will cut you into tiny pieces and scatter you to the winds."

Curiosity twines with their worry. "Fascinating. I expected most of your determination to be sheer stubbornness, but you genuinely have a connection with this human." They give themself a shake. "Very well. I'll be back at some point in the near future to check on the status of things. I highly recommend *you* tell her the truth. The full truth. She might surprise you."

"What does it matter if I be the one to tell her?"

"Trust me. It does."

That means less than nothing to me. "Goodbye,

Ramanu." I wait for them to teleport out before turning and walking back toward the staircase. It's easy for them to give advice when they're not in the midst of this. Not the way I am. Not the way Grace is.

I never would've chosen the way things fell out last night, not if I hadn't lost control. But the fact remains that Grace could have killed me and put an end to it . . . and she chose not to. I'm sure she had her reasons—I'm not naive enough to think that pure desire drove her—but I read her emotions, and desire was at the forefront in the bath last night.

I've already told her more about my family than I would've told a new acquaintance. She knows they're gone, and Ramanu disclosed plenty of the rest just now. What does it matter that the reason they're dead is because a human murdered them? That I didn't help them because I was too afraid? There's no reason to take a deep dive into my past trauma. It won't solve anything, and if she looks at me with pity or disgust, that might be the thing that finally breaks me.

Better to focus on the future.

Footsteps bring my head up in time to see Grace descending the stairs, a stubborn look on her face. I don't know what it says about me that I welcome the coming confrontation. I hold perfectly still and wait for her to reach me. It doesn't take long.

She stops several steps above me, leaving our faces almost even. "I think we got off to the wrong start."

That startles a laugh out of me. "What gave that impression?"

"I have no desire to fight you every day through the next seven years." She narrows her eyes at me, and I get that distinct impression that she's trying to read me. "I won't say

I'm not sympathetic to your situation, but under no circumstances am I having a child with you that I will leave in the demon realm."

Seven years gives me a long time to change her mind, but I get the feeling there's no changing the resolve coming off her in waves. That should be enough for me to take Azazel up on his offer to switch out Grace for another human who would be more accommodating. It's the smart thing to do. The action that will further my goals and get me out of this desperate situation.

I . . . don't want to.

"I'll get the birth control pendant for you today and explain how it works." I study her just as closely as she's studying me. "But I'm not going to stop trying to convince you to see things my way."

She flares a bright pink before she gets herself under control. My Grace seems to like the battle just as much as I'm starting to. I don't understand it. Up until this point, all my encounters with lovers had been soft, caring. At least until what happened to my family ensured I had no partners to choose from. There was never this fury, this willingness to draw a line and then promptly step over it in the name of dominance.

I don't know what it says about me that I crave it. I am actively looking forward to the next time Grace tries to slip away from me, to tracking her down and bringing her back, to the battle that will undoubtably play out in my bed.

"I'll gut you before I let that happen."

"Promises, promises." Though I get a perverse amount of enjoyment out of verbally sparring with this woman, I take a slow step back and lower my wings. Whether I'm enjoying it or not, we can't exist in a state of constant battle. The longer we bicker, the greater the chance of her storming off. I'm not ready to be alone again. "Are you hungry?"

She opens her mouth as if caught in the momentum of the argument but pauses when she seems to process what I just asked her. "I could eat."

"Let's see what Silas has put together for breakfast." I pivot and offer her my arm. I'm quietly pleased when she gives me a sharp look but slips her hand into the crook of my elbow. "The formal dining room is mostly for show. Unless you prefer it, I usually take my breakfasts and lunches in the kitchen."

"Meals in the kitchen sounds like more my speed." Grace very carefully doesn't look at me. "I'm not one to stand on ceremony, and the dining room table is way too formal for my tastes."

We pivoted so quickly, I don't know what to think. Maybe it's as simple as her not wanting to be alone any more than I do. I guide us through the echoing halls until we reach the kitchen. I thought I heard Silas cooking, but when we walk through the door, the room is empty.

There are two plates sitting on the kitchen counter. Waiting for us.

Grace eyes them with understandable distress. "Is this castle manned by ghosts?"

"Ghosts aren't real."

"Actually, they are." She has a strange look on her face. There's a flicker of white in her energy before she locks it down. Grief. "They're hellishly difficult to deal with. Salt is pretty much the only thing that works, and it's a temporary measure."

Again, I'm struck by the fact that this is no ordinary human. I may not have had interactions with more than a handful over the years, but Grace stands apart. I pull out her chair and wait for her to take a seat before I do the same. I know the proper thing to do in this situation. I should keep up the casual, safe small talk and allow Grace to get more comfortable with me. It feels like a lie.

Maybe that's why I say what I'm really thinking. "How is it that you came to be in contact with vampires? I was under the impression that they don't mingle with humans overmuch."

Grace takes a bite and chews slowly. "They don't. But my family has a, ah, special relationship with paranormals. We've been aware of them for as long as they've existed in our realm."

She's not saying anything I didn't already suspect, but I can't help pressing. "And you help them?"

"Sometimes." Grace pokes at her food. "Usually humans are the ones in desperate need of help, but there are exceptions to every rule."

If she [illegible]sn't know the various quirks and secrets that [illegible]g a gargoyle, it's probably in my best interest [illegible]er. It takes a lot of practice to hide emotions [illegible] can read them in the very air around you, [illegible]. With such a complicated human who is [illegible]eed every advantage I can get.

[illegible]gs feels too much like a lie in and of [illegible]

[illegible] read your energy. All gargoyles, all those with gargoyles in their family history, can. Each color has a different meaning, an emotion attached to it. You're not desperate. You haven't been desperate for a moment since I met you." The closest she got was when she was tangled in that web with the spiders closing in, but even that wasn't true desperation.

Grace twists to face me and frowns. "For a king or leader

or whatever the terminology is, you're absolute garbage at keeping secrets. Don't you know that you should hold every possible resource close? If I didn't know you could read my emotions, that would be an incredible weapon in your arsenal. And you just gave it away for nothing."

She is . . . angry? No, that's not quite right. She doesn't seem to know how to feel any more than I do. Her emotions flicker and swirl in a confusing maelstrom of colors. I look away to avoid getting dizzy. "That kind of thought process should only be used against enemies."

"That's naive and you know it. There's no way the gargoyles and the other people who inhabit this realm are that much different than humans. All I have to do is pick up a history book to see that allies can become enemies all too quickly when power is on the line."

She's right, but I still don't understand why she's so worked up over this. "That should be a relief to you. Maybe one of them will make a move soon and kill me, which will break the contract and send you back to the bargainer demon territory. That's what you want, isn't it?"

"Yes." The way she says it is almost a lie. Her energy doesn't quite change, but she won't meet my gaze, and she turns away. "Of course that's what I want."

I push my food away, no longer hungry. "Why are you here, Grace?" She opens her mouth to answer, but I press on before she can get any words out. "Not here in this castle. Not here with me. Here in the demon realm. What did Ramanu mean when they said Azazel has answers about your mother?"

"I told you already. I'm paying the price of someone else's deal."

The bullshit might've worked with me before, but it doesn't make sense with the things I know now. I shake my head sharply. "Don't you think I deserve to know the truth? I've given you the courtesy of being honest. Can't you do the same?" Even as I say it, I'm not sure I believe myself. Ultimately, she doesn't owe me anything. We might be in this together, but it's a temporary situation.

Grace uses her fork to move her food around her plate. Finally she sighs. "Okay, you might have a point. My mother is dead, and has been for some time, I think. It's been five years in the human realm, but time moves differently. Azazel is the only one who has the full story of what happened, and I want to know. I *need* to know."

"Why would Azazel have answers about your mother—" I realize the answer before I even finish speaking. Her mother made a demon deal and then never came home. And now Grace has moved across realms to get the answers she craves. Would I do any less if there were questions about how my family had died and I was the last one left? No wonder she is so determined to leave my side and make her way back to the bargainer demon territory.

If I were a better man, I would release her from the fucked-up bargain we put in place between us. If I were a worse one, I would use this knowledge to ensure her compliance with my needs and demands.

I do neither. Instead, I find myself studying her. "Would you like to see more of the lands around the castle? I'd like to get out of here for a bit and I wouldn't say no to some company."

She lifts her brows. "Playing hooky? Surely someone will come looking."

"These days the castle mostly runs itself and my company is hardly entertaining enough for most people to seek out."

"Bram . . ." She presses her lips together for a long

moment and then says, "I'd love to see the grounds around the castle."

She's likely only agreeing to better plan her next escape attempt, but I don't care. I'm happy to spend more time with her. I nudge her plate back toward her. "Eat up. You're going to want your strength for this."

12

BRAM

I almost talk myself out of taking Grace along half a dozen times before she meets me on the roof dressed in so many layers that she looks a bit like a child bundled against the cold. Or, well, a child of some other people. Gargoyles are naturally resistant to extreme temperatures, even from the time we're born.

I hold out my hand. "Shall we?"

"Do you have a destination in mind?"

I hadn't when I made the offer, but now I find myself saying, "There's an old keep in the mountains. It was used in my grandparents' generation, but it's falling into disrepair. I like to go out there regularly and make sure that it's still structurally sound because there's a superstition among my people that anyone who can spend an hour at midnight in the wine cellar without light will receive good luck and blessings."

Grace raises her brows. "Not that old of a superstition if it was still used two generations ago."

I understand how she sees things that way, but that's not how my people operate. I shrug. "Superstitions are living things, and sometimes they can shift in the space of a few decades. Other times, they stretch back through the years to beyond living memory."

Saying this the hot spring so high in the mountains that only the most reckless of people would normally attempt to reach it, where it's said that immersing yourself in the water will result in a healthy pregnancy and a safe birth. Several times a year, pilgrimages are organized to visit it. It doesn't matter how dangerous the trek—people always show up.

It seems foolhardy to me to risk life and limb in order to protect yourself from risking life and limb, but any faith I had died with my family.

Grace slips her hand into mine and allows me to lift her into my arms. She feels good there. If I didn't know better, I might believe she was built to occupy the space. I *do* know better, though. She might be indulging me now, but this is still the same woman who lied to me and then ran from me. She didn't talk to me about what she wanted or needed. She treated me like an obstacle to overcome.

Just like my people do.

I launch us into the air, flying far too quickly, as if I can outrace my dark thoughts. It's never worked before. It doesn't work now. And yet, they don't cling quite as harshly as they normally do. Strange, that.

We make good time to the keep, and I touch down softly in the courtyard just as the sun reaches its peak in the sky. Part of me wants to keep Grace in my arms, to use the excuse of her potential shakiness to do so, but she's much sturdier than she was last time. "You didn't scream."

"What?"

Why the fuck did I just say that? That's not a normal thing to say. Then again, this is not a normal woman. I set her carefully on her feet and keep my hands out in case her legs buckle.

Of course they don't. Which means I have no excuse to avoid answering her question. I look away and fight not to hunch my shoulders. "The first time we flew. You were scared. But you didn't scream. You didn't scream with the spiders, either."

"Oh." She absently combs her fingers through her windswept hair. "It's training. One of the first things I learned as a kid was to not make a noise when I'm scared. Silence is a prey instinct that humans don't have for some reason. Too often we scream and bring the predator right to us. My family was invested in ensuring that I didn't get myself or anyone else killed."

Because they save people. I don't know if that's the full explanation for her knowledge and instincts. Saving people sounds like a virtuous activity. I can't imagine how one trains a child not to make a sound when they're afraid. I glance at her face, but her expression and her energy invite no further questions on the subject.

That's okay. I may not be good at dodging the dark things that plague my steps, but I can try. Right now. For her.

I turn to the keep. It appears much the same as it did the last time I was here a few weeks ago. Weathered gray stone that looks downright immortal, the building carved right into the side of the mountain. The only true sign of decay is the tower that has crumbled to nothing, beaten down by the winds that howl through this ravine.

Grace whistles softly. "I can see why this place is a test of bravery. It's creepy as shit."

"There are no ghosts here." At least not ones she would recognize. I'm young for my people, barely forty, so I was born well after we descended from the heights and built the castle that I live in now. My father used to talk about this place fondly when I was younger, some of the few times he seemed like someone I could understand. I can't see it the way he saw it. Supposedly this is a happy place. But when war came, it was too isolated to properly defend. It might have been okay if our main opponents in that conflict were the dragons or the kraken, but the succubi and incubi can fly. It only took one devastating attack before there was a call for a change in location. My grandparents headed it, and as a leader, I absolutely understand why they did.

But, as I stand here beside Grace, listening to the wind howl and scream, I feel significantly more at peace than I ever am in the castle in the lower reaches.

Grace turns to me with a mischievous look in her eyes. "Can I see the wine cellar? I could use some good luck."

"It's a superstition, not a fact."

"Come on, Bram." She turns around to face me as she walks backward toward the door. "You're a magic man with wings, horns, and the ability to see auras. You, more than anyone, should be willing to believe in magic."

I follow her as if she wrapped a string around my heart and tugged. I haven't known this woman long, but this is the side of her that I never expected. It's almost playful, with a reckless edge that I recognize all too well. If I don't accompany her, she'll still go down to the basement and she might hurt herself along the way. "We can go, but you have to promise to be careful."

"Absolutely not. Where's the fun in that?" She grins. "But if it's going to stress you out, I suppose you can lead the way. "

The castle may be made of stone, but it wasn't built to be accessible to those without wings. There are stairs and ways to get around without flying, but they're tucked out of the main hallways. This is one of the biggest changes that was made to the design for the castle I live in now. A welcome one, honestly. It's ridiculous to require someone with a wing injury or disability—or wingless guests—to go so far out of the way. I'm glad it's no longer an issue.

But it gives me the excuse to launch forward and scoop Grace into my arms again. I enjoy her snarl of faux outrage. "No stairs. We'll take the fast way."

"The—" She lets out a little yip as I step through the door and right off the ledge into the air shaft below.

I like that sound. I like it even more now because I know she's not actually scared. We descend in a lazy spiral, finally coming to land three floors below. This time, I'm slower to set Grace on her feet. "Be careful. Some of the ceiling has started to collapse in certain areas."

She turns a slow circle, taking everything in with her gray eyes that see far too much. "This place is remarkably well-preserved. I'm surprised you bother to do sweeps of it. People can be fools, but I would think most of them could navigate this space without too much trouble."

Something akin to embarrassment heats my skin. I drag my hands through my hair and look away, unable to meet her gaze. "There's not a lot of help my people accept from me. Each of the noble families is responsible for their own portion of the territory, and while I technically oversee all of them, they've been functioning well for generations and don't require much oversight. There's only so many territories in this realm, and I've already negotiated the trade deals that benefit us. Those will continue to remain in place unless something drastic happens. "Patrolling the spaces where superstitions lead my people and ensuring there are no dangers here?" I lift my hands and let them fall back to my sides. "It's the least I could do."

She props her hands on her hips. "Bram, I don't know if

that's the single sweetest thing you've ever said, or the saddest. It's quite possibly both."

The flashing feeling beneath my skin gets stronger. "It's what anyone would do in my position."

"No. It's really not." She makes a move as if she's about to shift toward me but seems to think better of it. "Most people wouldn't dredge up the effort to piss on the nobles if they were on fire after the way they turned on you. Most people would punish them for the disrespect. Most people would use their power as leader of the territory to force obedience. Or maybe walk away completely. I don't know. Either way, they wouldn't continue to care for people who repeatedly reject them."

The way she says that . . . it's almost as if she admires it. But that can't be right. I've fallen short of every expectation set for me. That trend started long before my family died and my cowardice ensured my survival. I was always too soft for my father's tastes. I can still feel his derision, can see the colors painted across the air around him. "You're wrong. I'm nothing special."

Grace is silent for several beats. I refuse to look at her, refuse to see her colors and what they might tell me. Finally, she says, "If you say so. Now, show me the space that will bring me luck."

Gratitude flows through me. I'm glad she's not pressing the issue. I might feel a kinship with this woman, but the truth is that we're barely more than strangers. Whatever she thinks she knows about me, she doesn't. I clear my throat. "It only brings luck if you're down here at midnight."

"Maybe. But from what you said, it's a new superstition. Maybe your people just haven't explored the full parameters of it."

Despite myself, I smile a little. "Maybe."

I lead her down the hall to the wine cellar—a long, deep room carved right out of the mountain. There are no windows, and the temperature drops several degrees as we step inside. Good for wine. Less so for humans sensitive to the cold. "It looks fine. Let's go before you catch a chill."

"Are you worried about me, Bram?" A pale flicker of orange shows her surprise. "I appreciate the concern, but a little cold won't hurt me." She moves deeper into the room and tilts her head back, then closes her eyes. "I see why they come here. It might be creepy as shit, but it's a little peaceful, too. You can barely hear the wind. It feels a little like you're the last person left in this realm."

I move closer despite myself, drawn by the strange peace emanating from her. "Doesn't the thought of being the last person left scare you?"

"No," she says simply. "I've been alone for five years now. Long enough to get good at it. But if I'm the last person left" —she reaches out and takes my hand—"or, for the sake of argument, we're the last two people left? It means no one needs to be saved. No one needs to be ruled. No one needs us at all. And yeah, there's a part of me that finds that really attractive."

Understanding curls through me. How many times has she said or done something that immediately resonates with me? She's a stranger, and yet I feel like I know her down to her very bones. I squeeze her hand, close my eyes, and tilt my head back, mimicking her posture. "That is really attractive, isn't it?"

Just the two of us left alone in the world.

It's not reality, but I stand here in the dark, in silence, and share the fantasy with her. At least for a little while.

13

GRACE

I don't know what I'm doing. If I had half a brain in my head, I would wait for Bram to lower his guard before attempting another escape. I would stack the deck in my favor as much as possible. I would ensure I had supplies enough to last me a week at least. I would do a lot of things.

I don't do any of it.

It feels cliché to say today changed things. It didn't. It *can't*. Except . . . I get him a little better than I did before. I see him clearer.

I want him more.

I wait for the dead of night, and then I slip out of the castle using a different door than I did before. It doesn't matter. I'm certain I can feel his eyes on me. I don't head toward the lake—there's not even a hint of an exit route that direction—but to the fields in the east. It's a garbage tactical decision when my pursuer can take to the air.

I look over my shoulder into the sky, but it's too dark, and the cloud cover hides everything from view. He could be directly overhead and I would never know it, not until he dived down and took me. Anticipation curls through me.

Unforgivable, and yet it's the truth. I pick up my pace until I'm jogging over the uneven ground. The tree line is to my right, but I'm not prepared to go there yet. The forest is all but impossible to navigate in the dark, and I don't relish the idea of being caught in those webs again.

This is so foolish, I can't even put it into words. *What am I doing?*

My only answer is a faint whistling sound. I barely register it at first. Then my instincts catches up to my brain, and I sprint toward the trees. It's already too late.

Between one step and the next, rough hands hook under my armpits and wrench me into the air. The ground disappears beneath my feet as Bram cuts upward. Then the motherfucker tosses me, and I'm weightless for one horrifying breath before he catches me in his arms. At first, I think he might have done it to get a better grip on me, but as he turns for the castle, he does it again. He drops me, letting me fall for several seconds, then catches me again and takes us higher. Only to repeat the process again. Through it all, I don't scream. I can't tell if I'm afraid or furious or, gods help me, turned on.

I still don't have an answer when he dives through a large window toward the top of the castle. I'm shaking, and I can't seem to stop. There's no way my legs will hold me. They don't have to. Bram tosses me onto his bed and plasters a massive hand on my chest when I start to sit up. "I told you the consequences of your actions."

Yeah, he really did. Knowing that I chose this is somehow all the more humiliating. I shouldn't have been looking forward to the moment when he caught me and dragged me back. And yet here I am, thighs pressed together, breathlessly waiting to see what he'll do next.

Wait, what am I doing? I saw how he reacted in the bath,

and I know how I felt the moment I took control. Who's to say I can't do that now?

He's dressed much the same as he has been since I met him, his stony skin mostly bare except for a loincloth sort of thing wrapped around his hips. After the chance to get acquainted with his cock last night, the possibilities of those ridges made me lose sleep. In fact, he's so hard, I can clearly see the ridges outlined against the fabric of the loincloth. First things first, though. I sit up. "The birth control pendant?"

"So eager for my cock, aren't you?" He moves away from the bed. His wing lashes out, and the spur catches something on a nearby dresser that I hadn't noticed before. He tosses it in my lap. It's exactly what I imagined it would be: a pendant on a chain with some arcane writing on it that I can't decipher. Back in my realm, there are a thousand and one magical ways to magically ensure no pregnancy occurs during sexual encounters. And they all have fewer side effects than prescription medication.

This could be a trap.

"How does it work?"

He doesn't move. He doesn't seem to even breathe. "You need a little of your blood to activate it and key it to you. After that, as long as you're wearing it, you can't conceive."

I wait for the catch, but he doesn't say anything else. He doesn't have to. As I search his aura, I find not even the slightest hint of deception. That doesn't mean it's not there, but if Bram is a liar, he's the best I've ever met. My instincts are rarely incorrect when it comes to identifying threats, and if Bram is a threat, it's not because he's trying to trap me.

He hasn't bothered to hide what he wants, and though he orchestrated this devil's bargain between us when I was under duress, that doesn't mean I'm not willing. Quite the contrary. I've all but waved a red flag in front of him and demanded he chase me.

That's why I don't hesitate to slice my finger and press it to the pendant. The effect is instantaneous. It pulses, and I feel an answering pulsing low in my stomach. "Is there some kind of waiting period?"

"No."

Thank the gods. I don't care if this is a terrible idea. I don't care if this man is a godsawful match for me. I certainly don't care that he makes me act in a way that's in direct counterpoint to my goals. Terrifying though it may be, when I'm with him, I feel less alone. When we go toe-to-toe, there's no room for the old grief that has plagued my steps, for the worry about a future in which all I can see is yet more loneliness, followed by an early death. Who will bury me when some monster I'm hunting strikes me down? I have no family left. Likely I will get some gravestone in a generic human cemetery, with the name "Jane Doe" written across the stone.

I don't have to think about that now. In fact, I don't have to think about that for the next seven years if I don't want to. It might mean waiting for answers, but I've already waited years. What are a few more? Guilt threatens to sink its claws into to me at the thought, but I don't have to let it.

At least not tonight.

"Take off your clothes, Bram."

"You first." His eyes rake over my body so intensely that I swear I can feel them. "I want to see you." But he doesn't move an inch closer. He won't until I give him permission . . . until I *order* him. Again, that intoxicating power flows through me. I might not have control of my life or my destiny, but right now, in this bedroom, I have control of

Bram. It's willingly given, which makes this sensation all the more intoxicating.

"No," I say slowly. "After that little stunt you pulled outside, you have to earn my body. The first step is removing your clothing." When he still hesitates, I tilt my head to the side. "You know how this game is played, Bram. If you want it to end, all you need to do is tell me to stop. You can walk out the door, and I won't do a thing to keep you here. I certainly won't hold it against you."

He snorts. "You're in my room, Grace."

"Yes, I am. And the moment this ends, I will go back to my room." I fight not to hold my breath, not to let him know how desperately I need his obedience. His submission.

Is his breath coming a little faster? It's hard to tell, but I think it is. He licks his lips. "If I play this game with you, where will we end tonight?"

He wants this just as much as I do. He's the one who orchestrated the events that brought me to this place. To this sexual bargain. He's the one who desperately wants to hit his knees and give himself over to me. I just need to give him one last little push. An excuse to take what he wants . . . or, rather, to allow me to give it to him. To fulfill his needs.

I drag my finger along the chain of the birth control pendant slowly. He tenses, almost as if he's fighting not to pounce on me. The thought gives me a thrill. He won't. I'm certain of it. Not until I give the command. "If you play this game with me, if you submit to my commands like the good boy that I know you can be, then we will end tonight with me riding your cock." I lean forward, and he mirrors the movement. My body goes tight, and I lower my voice, coaxing him closer still. "And if you're very, *very* good, I'll let you fill me up."

His nostrils flare. Without leaning away or creating any

farther distance between us, he reaches down and unwraps the cloth shielding him from my sight. It hits the floor with barely a sound. I don't think either of us is breathing. It feels like a gunshot went off.

I lean back and prop myself up on my hands so I can watch him to my heart's content. Truth be told, I need him to touch me just as much as I need to touch him. But there is delicious agony in making us both wait. I knew Bram was well-built. I had his cock in my hands and mouth a very short time ago. It doesn't matter. The sight of him makes me clench my thighs together.

There's no reason to hold off this time. I don't have to stop myself from riding his cock. With this pendant around my neck, the worst consequence is out of reach. If my heart is a little more tender than I expected, it's a small enough price to pay for an escape with this man. One that will benefit both of us.

"Kneel."

Bram doesn't hesitate. He lowers himself slowly to the floor and arranges himself on his knees. If I didn't know better, I would think he had some kind of training in the submissive arts because he spreads his thighs just enough to frame his cock and balls and drapes his wings behind him, pretty as a picture. But then I look at his face and realize it's not intentional at all. He's moving on automatic, every bit of his focus narrowed on me.

It's more intoxicating than any drug I've tried. I want more. Now.

I sit up a little and pull my shirt over my head. I didn't bother with anything underneath it. Not when I knew where we'd end up tonight. I'm not about to give away everything for a simple command, but I do pause to toe off my boots and socks.

"You're very beautiful. You know that, don't you?" I eye the slope of his shoulders and the thick slices of muscle moving beneath his cool skin. "Whatever creator you believe in spent a little extra time when forming you."

His aura swirls with the magenta of embarrassment and the deep fuchsia of pleasure. "You don't have to say things like that to me."

"I don't have to do anything I don't want to do, Bram. I like complimenting you. It's the truth, and it pleases me to see you squirm." I drift my fingers down my chest to cup one breast. He forgets all about his embarrassment as he watches me circle my nipple with my thumb. "I know you don't have a high opinion of yourself, but I would like to hear you tell me your greatest strength."

He shakes his head sharply. "That's nonsense. What does such a thing matter?"

"I suppose what it matters is up to you." I trail my fingers further, down my stomach to the top of my pants. "I'll happily remove these . . . just as soon as you answer my question honestly."

14

BRAM

I knew that there would be bedroom games played tonight, but I didn't expect Grace to fuck with my head so thoroughly. Or so quickly. She's serious too. I can read her resolve in the violet of her energy. She knows how uncomfortable this makes me, but she's not going to relent.

I grit my teeth and force the words out. "My greatest strength is my strength itself."

"Wrong. Try again."

I glare, but my ire seems to bounce right off her. Worse, she's still playing with the top of her pants, and I can barely think past the promise of seeing her pretty pussy again. I swallow hard. I can do this. I can cut myself open and lay myself bare for her. "My greatest strength is my loyalty. Once I give it, I will not waver." I might fail to do what needs to be done, but I'll *want* to do the right thing. I don't know if that makes my loyalty better or worse.

"Very good. Very, very good."

It's everything I can do to keep myself still as she lifts her hips and works her pants down her legs. She kicks the pants off the rest of the way and parts her legs. I've never wished so fervently for bright light. The moonlight coming in through the open window is nowhere near enough to illuminate her to my satisfaction. Even so, I see her clearly.

Her toned thighs, peppered with scars from the life she never talks about. Her perfect pink pussy, a delight I fully intend to enjoy to the fullest before the night's over. *But only if I'm good.* The thought sends goose bumps over my entire body and makes my cock strain. I don't know how she manages to collar me with so few words, but I feel like she has her hand wrapped around my throat.

I fucking love it.

"Oh, Bram. You try so hard to be the monster you believe you are, but right down at the core of you, you are an honorable man. Maybe even too honorable."

That startles a harsh laugh out of me. "Hardly."

"Too honorable by far." Her fingers coast over her belly button and then lower, skating around to stroke first one thigh and then the other. "If you weren't, you would've brought the nobles in your territory to their knees by now. If you weren't"—she presses on as if she can see me about to protest—"then you would've taken what you want from me by now."

"Just because I want you willingly coming on my cock doesn't mean I have honor, Grace. Don't mistake me."

"I wouldn't dream of it." Finally, what feels like an eternity later, she creates a V with her fingers and parts her pussy. "Don't move until I tell you to."

It's as if she's reached across the distance and turned me to stone right down to my bones. I watch in helpless desire and frustration as she strokes her clit in small circles. I remember exactly the pattern she likes, the one that I used with my tongue to make her come all over my face last night. It's the same she's using now.

She dips her fingers down and presses two inside her. I actually let out a groan as I witness them disappear into the space I desperately need to occupy. She doesn't fuck herself with them, though. She merely spreads her wetness back up to her clit and resumes stroking herself. It's only a minute or two later when her head falls back and her breasts heave with her harsh breathing.

Holy fuck, she's going to make herself come.

Without letting me touch her.

"Grace." My voice is a ragged plea. "Let me. Please."

She lifts her head just enough to meet my gaze. Gods, but she's stunning. The command and her gray eyes hold me captive more thoroughly than any bonds could. "Do *not* move." The words are soft, but no less of an order for their lack of volume.

I press my hands hard to my thighs as she continues to stroke herself. I've never been one to come fast, and certainly not without some sort of physical stimulation, but as her thighs start to shake and her fingers coat with her desire, I am suddenly terrified that I'm about to orgasm without touching my cock at all.

The hold this woman has on me is borderline witchcraft. Except that's a cop-out. It's not magic that ties me to Grace, or at least it's not magic beyond the demon bargain we both made. It's a kinship that I've never felt with another person. It defies belief, but somehow this woman is broken in exactly the same way I am. The fault lines on her soul are a perfect match for mine.

"Oh, fuck." She presses hard on her clit. And then a single word slips from her lips, so soft that I almost convince myself I'm hearing things. I must be. Surely she didn't just whisper my name as she came.

I can't move. I can't think. I am a receptacle for her demand, so when she crooks her finger at me, I know exactly what she requires without her saying anything at all. I crawl to her. It's not a long distance, but it's incredibly awkward with my wings. It should be demeaning; in fact, it is.

I've never felt so at peace.

I stop at the edge of the bed. She's so close, it would take no effort at all to touch her. I know better than that. From the twist of Grace's lips, she understands exactly how much it cost me to keep my hands to my thighs as she came.

She sits up, a little awkward in her desire-drugged movements. "That was an excellent appetizer." Grace leans forward and eyes my cock. "Are you in pain?"

"Always. I can handle it."

Now she truly smiles. Her approval warms me as if it were the sun itself. I actually have to close my eyes against it. But I open them just as quickly because I don't want to miss a minute of this.

Grace catches my jaw. "You did well. But now I'm all messy. Would you like to clean me up?"

There was only ever going to be one answer to this question. I am nearly certain I might die if I don't taste her again. Clean her up? I want to make a mess of us both. I nod slowly. "Yes."

"I thought so." She pinches my jaw lightly, guiding my mouth open. Then she presses her fingers, still wet with her orgasm, between my lips. A shiver racks my body. Can a person die of bliss? Before tonight, I would've said it was impossible. Now I'm not so sure.

I try to close my mouth around her fingers to suck her

clean, but her grip on my jaw goes hard. We both know there's nothing she's doing to me that I did not consent to. But I still make a sound of protest.

Grace raises her brows. "Would you like me to stop?"

What I want is for her to go harder, deeper. But I can't say that with her fingers in my mouth. She seems to realize it the same moment I do. Grace slowly withdraws her fingers almost completely, pausing only when the tips of them meet my bottom lip. "Well?"

"No, I don't want you to stop." I swallow hard, tasting her on my tongue.

"If you change your mind—"

"I won't."

She tightens her grip on my jaw and pulls me in to place a devastatingly gentle kiss on my lips. "If you change your mind, tell me. That *is* a command, by the way." Then her fingers are back in my mouth. This time, she's not as gentle. She holds me immobile and fucks my mouth with her fingers. All the while she stares deep into my eyes as if she can see my very soul. As if she's daring me to buckle, to do anything other than enjoy what she's doling out.

Enjoy, I do.

I've never felt so owned. I never knew that was something I could crave. Not just the domination, though that gets me so hard, it feels like my cock might burst. It's in the caring too. She doesn't just want me on my knees. She wants me there willingly. She wants me enjoying this just as much as she is, playing this game all the way until completion. I've never felt so vulnerable and yet so cared for.

When I can no longer taste her on her fingers, she eases them from my mouth. "Now the rest." There's no mistaking her words, especially when she leans back and once again spreads her thighs. I make a sound that's almost a sob of relief. And then I lean down and press my mouth to her pussy. I'm shaking. The first lick of her center is divine. I can't seem to stop.

At least until she takes her fingers into my hair and pulls hard. "Was I not clear?" There's a dangerous edge to her tone. "I didn't tell you to fuck me with your tongue, Bram. I told you to clean up my mess."

Again, that sound that's part sob and part whimper slips free. It takes far more effort than I could've dreamed to move back and start licking her thighs. She keeps her hand in my hair, guiding me to each new spot and holding me there until I finish my task.

Oh fuck, I really might come.

Especially when I'm finally allowed to reach her pussy and lap at her there. Not her clit—she doesn't allow me that pleasure—but everywhere else. I might have died of desperation if not for the little tremors that work through her body, letting me know this is just as much agony for her as it is for me.

She finally lightens her grip enough that I can press my forehead to her lower stomach. I'm breathing as if I've just flown for miles and miles without a break. Her thighs shake on either side of my head, but her voice is almost normal. "That was . . . adequate."

"I can do better." I don't know where the words come from, only that they're the truth.

"Next time." She tugs on my hair again. "Come here."

I allow her to guide me until our faces are even. Grace releases my hair and cups my face with her shaking hands. And then she kisses me. It's not soft and sweet like last time. No, this is a declaration of ownership. She possesses my mouth, and I am only too happy to submit. I want to wrap her up and pull her close until I don't know where she ends and I begin. I need her so desperately that I dig my fingers into my thighs again to prevent myself from disobeying her. *Holy fuck, what is* happening *to me?*

She only breaks the kiss when we're both trembling. Grace leans back just a little. "On the bed. On your back." With my wings pinned beneath me.

She knows what she's asking me. She knows what I'm giving her by obeying.

I don't hesitate. I stand on shaking legs and move around her to lie back on my bed. Without her saying a word, I reach my arms over my head and grip the thick stone headboard. I'm not restrained in any true way, but I am helpless before her all the same.

She kneels between my thighs and drags her nails over them. "Another time, I would make you hold this position while I pleasured you until you couldn't take it anymore."

Another time, I would love that. If she tried that right now, I would only last about thirty seconds. Grace knows it too. She stops stroking me and moves to straddle my hips. "I need you too much to play that game right now. But I need to make one thing clear, Bram. Are you listening?"

I'm having a hard time focusing on anything other than her pussy, hovering bare inches above my straining cock. I swallow hard. "Yes, I'm listening."

"Keep your hands on the headboard, or I'll stop what I'm doing. Do you understand?"

She wants me *not* to touch her while she's touching me so intimately. She's giving me both pleasure and agony with the restriction. I nod jerkily. "Yes. I understand."

15

GRACE

Being with Bram is like experiencing a fever dream, and yet I've never felt more aware. There's power in his submission, in the gift he's made of it. Perched on his hips, with his perfect body laid out for my pleasure, I have another moment of wondering if I've bitten off more than I can chew. He's so *big* in every way.

I've never let fear make my decisions for me, and I'm not about to start now.

I move up his broad chest to kiss him again. I love kissing this man. Sometimes it's a battle, and sometimes, like right now, it's like falling from a high place into strong arms that will always catch me. All my life, I've been told to trust no one but family. I haven't trusted Bram with every one of my secrets, but I've trusted him with my life and my body. That's no small thing.

And now he's trusting me with his.

I straighten a little and plant my hands on his stomach, pinning his cock between us. I truly don't know if I can take him, but a little more lubrication can't hurt. Not to mention that I've been dying to feel his ridges ever since I discovered them. I roll my hips, grinding along the length of his cock. It's even better than I hoped. "Oh, *fuck*."

"Grace." The muscles in his arms are so tense that I can trace every line. I'm honestly surprised the headboard hasn't cracked under the force of his grip. His voice rumbles in his chest like rocks grating together. "If you keep doing that, this will be over before I can get inside you."

I love his honesty just as much as I love how deeply I affect him. It's only right that I reward both of us for getting this far. "I'll make you a bargain, Bram."

He narrows his eyes even as he pants with need. "It's a little late for bargains."

"You know better. It's never too late for bargains." I roll my hips, and I can't help my little gasp as my clit finds a particularly pleasurable ridge. He might be worried about coming too fast, but I'm already on the edge again. It's never been like this with me, this almost frenzy barely concealed under a veneer of dominance. "Hold out until I come all over your cock. If you do, I'll let you fuck me however you desire."

"However I desire?" He curses long and hard, making me clench my thighs around him. "That's a tempting offer."

"Let's see if you can live up to it." I rise onto my knees only to discover that it's not enough height. Holy fuck, I really don't know if I can do this. It doesn't matter. I have to try.

I get my feet under me and crouch over him. Only then can I position his cock in my entrance. The size difference feels obscene like this. Something almost like true fear flickers inside me. "I don't know if I can take you."

"You can." He says it with such confidence, I wonder if he's had human lovers in the past. I'm not prepared for the jealousy I feel in response to that thought. Bram shifts beneath me. "No, I've never fucked humans before, but plenty of my people have. It's possible. I promise it's possible."

I try to press down on his crown, but he's too broad to easily slip inside me. "*How?* This is impossible!"

"Grace." He rumbles my name. It's part command and part plea. "You just need a little more preparation. Let me. Please."

Desperation overrides any kind of Dominance/submission game we're playing. "Yes. Okay. Do it now."

I expect him to flip me and take control. He doesn't. He releases the headboard with one hand and positions it near his hip, palm up. "Ride my fingers."

His fingers are impressive, but they're still nowhere near the size of his cock. I need him too much to argue, though. I shift enough to press his fingers to my pussy. Again, Bram doesn't take control. Not really. He presses his middle finger inside me and holds steady as I ride it. It feels good. Really good. But it's only a few moments before it's not enough. "More."

He obediently offers me a second finger. This time, as I descend, I have to go slower to adjust. Especially when he's pressing against my walls, stretching me even more. Pleasure wraps around me. If he doesn't stop doing that, I'm going to come. I reach for his cock, but he shakes his head. "No. I'm hanging on by a thread. Come as many times as you need to, Grace."

The pads of his fingers pressing against my G-spot takes any hesitation away from me. I give myself over to fucking his fingers, riding them the way I desperately want to ride his cock. My orgasm blooms, closer and closer, but I fight it off with everything I have. *Not yet.*

Then he wedges a third finger into me.

I freeze. I was uncomfortably full with two. Three is almost painful. "Wait."

"You have control. Give yourself time. When you're ready, take what you need." He speaks softly, coaxingly. He soothes me with his words and tone even as it feels like he might rip me apart with his fingers.

But only for a moment. My body adjusts slowly, increment by increment. The lust that floods me is deep enough to drown in. "*Bram*."

"That's it. Just like that."

I barely register my body beginning to move. I don't make a conscious choice to do it. Instinct takes over. Tiny little tremors slowly morph into strokes. And still he stretches me. But that near pain is gone. All that's left is pleasure. Bram shifts and presses his palm to my clit. It feels so good that I panic and grab his wrist. "Wait." I'm panting just as hard as he is, and I'm so wet that I swear he's soaked to the wrist. "I don't want to come until it's your cock inside me."

"It would be better if you did."

Maybe he's right. Maybe he's not. I don't care. "I need your cock."

Bram tenses, and then suddenly I'm in the air, being lifted by my fucking pussy until I'm back crouching over his cock. Only then does he withdraw his fingers. He's the one who guides his broad cock to my entrance. This time, what felt impossible is merely a devastating challenge. I sink down, taking an inch of him inside me. *Holy fuck*.

Every inch is a battle between his body and mine. It feels too good to stop, but I can't slide all the way to the hilt in a smooth motion like I'd love to. My descent happens in fits and starts. By the time I seal us together completely, we're both covered in sweat and breathing as if we just ran a marathon.

"Fuck, fuck, fuck." I can't stop shaking. I need to move, but it's as if my bones have turned to jelly. My knees reach the bed now, but they won't if I try to lift myself all the way off him. "Bram—"

Somehow, he knows what I need before I get the words out. He reaches down and slides his hands under my knees. It seems impossible that he can keep me lifted indefinitely, but he doesn't hesitate to raise me into the air a few inches, creating a solid base for me to leverage myself on. The move makes every muscle in his torso stand out, and I shiver at the sight . . . which only makes me more aware of the way he fills me.

Slowly, carefully, I begin to move.

It's the most excruciating pleasure I've ever experienced. Every move has his ridges rubbing against delicious parts of me. I can barely keep my eyes open, but closing them means missing the way Bram watches me. Like a devout man who's finally seen the face of his god. Later, it might make me uncomfortable. Right now, I soak up his attention, revel in this moment of perfect understanding.

My body adjusts. It just takes a little longer than I'm used to. I roll my hips slowly, both because it feels good and because of how closely he watches me. His jaw is clenched so tightly, I worry for his teeth. "Bram."

"Come for me, Grace. Please. I can't—"

It's as if his desperation undoes my own. I pick up my pace, chasing that burning ember of need deep inside me. It flares hotter and hotter. So close . . . I could hold out. Maybe. Could wring him dry and win this little wager.

I don't want to.

I press my fingers to my clit, circling exactly the way I

need as I ride him. One stroke. Two. On the third, my body clenches so hard, it makes me dizzy. "Oh, *fuck*." I grind down on his cock, riding the wave that rises and rises until I'm suddenly terrified it will never crest. When it does, I almost black out.

Bram releases my knees, causing his cock to sink even deeper. I shriek, but the sound is cut off when he sits up and kisses me. He *clings* to me, his mouth moving against mine even as his hips pump into me. It's soft and sweet and . . . Oh fuck, I'm coming again.

This time, he follows me. His cock *pulses* inside me. I cry out again against his lips, and he swallows the sound even as he orgasms. On and on and on, each stroke a surge I can feel until his seed overflows and spills down my thighs and all over his lap.

I collapse against him, or maybe he collapses against me. I honestly can't be sure. We hold each other, shivering and shaking and weaving like two drunken sailors cast adrift in seas beyond our knowing.

At some point, I become aware of Bram brushing featherlight kisses along my throat and shoulder. His arms tighten around me. "Are you okay?"

"Yes." I think so. I'm going to be sore tomorrow, but the ache starting between my thighs is more than worth the cost of what I just experienced. I brush his hair back. "Are you?"

"No." He huffs out a rough laugh. "I think my world just tilted on its axis."

Yes. That's exactly what it feels like. I just didn't expect him to admit as much out loud. I kiss his temple, his horns. "You did well."

He makes a sound that's nearly a moan. "Give me a few moments and . . ."

"A bath." I kiss his brows. "Nice long hot soak. Then a

snack and a cuddle." I can barely move, but we're due for a crash, and I don't want to experience it alone. I don't want *him* to experience it alone. "How does that sound?"

Bram's arms tighten around me, and then he seems to make an effort to ease his hold. "That sounds good, Grace. Really, really good."

We manage to stagger to the bathroom and get the water running, though we barely last a few minutes before Bram is snoring softly, his head leaned back and his throat exposed. It was such a short time ago that he handed me a knife and pressed it to his throat, and now he bares the same vulnerability to me, but it feels like trust instead of a dare.

I wake Bram up and we muddle through drying off and stumbling to bed. He doesn't hesitate to wrap a big arm around my waist and tuck me in against his body. I probably shouldn't read into the fact that he falls asleep almost immediately, once again trusting me not to take advantage of his vulnerability.

I . . . like him. I don't know why that's such a revelation. I already knew I understood him. I just didn't expect to like him so much, even though part of me recognizes an identical part of him. I don't know what it means. Maybe it shouldn't mean anything at all.

I just don't know.

16

GRACE

I don't know why I keep putting myself in this position. I knew last night was a mistake before I ever left the castle. If some large part of me relished the chase, knowing I wouldn't escape . . . I don't know what to say to that. I wanted an excuse to be in Bram's bed, to truly explore everything he has to offer. I don't know what it says about me that I needed an excuse. If I wanted him, I should've been able to take him. But that's not how I operate.

I am a Jaeger.

We don't die of old age, and we are all too aware of the possibility of monsters wearing human skin. Sex makes everyone vulnerable—you're not protecting your throat when you're in the heart of an orgasm. Several members of my extended family were taken out like that. My mother called it a lesson to be heeded. She liked to make lessons out of a lot of things.

Pleasure is a lie. Happiness is fleeting. In the end, all we have is family.

I don't even have that anymore.

What I'm left with are questions I'm starting to wonder if

I'll ever get answers to. Oh, I believe Azazel and Ramanu when they claim they will give me the answers I seek. That's the problem, though. They might be able to tell me how my mother died and what she bargained for, but even if I know the terms of the deal she made with Azazel, will I know *why*?

It's the *why* that haunts me. She gave no indication of her plans. One day she was there, and the next she was simply gone, never to return. It wasn't for money. We have plenty of that, thanks to some clever investments made by my grandfather. It was all for . . . That's the thing. Nothing actually changed. It's not like she gave her life and we have something to show for it. She disappeared, leaving a gaping hole behind her. I want to know why, and I'm not sure I'll ever have that answer.

I certainly won't find it in Bram's bed.

And yet I can't quite make myself move. He's a warm presence at my side, with one heavy arm draped over my torso. It feels . . . nice. I'm sore but pleasantly so. His steady breathing soothes something in me; it's a sensation similar to when I stand on the beach and listen to the tide come in. I could live like this. I could spend the next seven years playing games with this man and ending up in his bed over and over. I could ride out my time until the bargainer demons share the information I came here to find.

It's shocking how tempting that is. If I just give in and stop fighting, maybe I'll get a little peace. The problem is that I don't know how to stop fighting. I've been doing it my entire life. Now that I'm the last Jaeger left, happily sharing the bed of a monster feels like a betrayal. It doesn't matter that none of the relatives whose opinion I valued would classify Bram as an actual monster. Not when he cares so much, is so willing to let me take the lead, and ensures that I am right there with him every step of the way.

But old habits die hard. I don't know how to just relax and enjoy this. I keep waiting for the bad thing to happen, even if I don't know what that bad thing is in this situation.

"Will we be fighting today or fucking . . . or both?"

I jolt. I hadn't even realized he was awake. His breathing certainly didn't change and give me any indication. Then his words penetrate. *Both?* "This will never work. I need answers, and you need a baby. We're both destined for disappointment."

"Most likely." He agrees so damned easily that it irks me. I know Bram cares deeply about his people; if he didn't, he would just leave them to the inevitable civil war that would occur upon his passing. *How can he care so much and yet be so defeatist?*

I didn't realize I spoke out loud until he answers me. He pulls me closer and tucks his face against my throat. "It's easy. When life kicks you in the teeth enough times, you learn to expect it. If I were any smarter, I would've given up fighting by now. Maybe I would have some peace then."

Every time he says shit like this, my heart feels like it's twisting in my chest. I dig my fingers into his hair and pull until he lifts his face and meets my gaze. "Stop that. If you were going to give up, you would've done it by now. You obviously have no intention of doing so, so stop with the dramatics."

"You call *me* dramatic?" His lips curve, but his eyes stay oh so serious. "You're the one who keeps fleeing into the night, chasing . . . I honestly don't even know what you're chasing at this point. What will it matter if you get answers now or in seven years? Will it change anything?"

I hate him a little bit for the question. Because he's right yet also so far off the mark that I want to set something on fire. "You can't honestly expect me to sit around and play with you for seven years when I know there are answers within reach."

"I don't." He sits up, easily breaking my hold on him. Truth be told, I don't try very hard to maintain it. Bram climbs off the bed and shakes out his wings with a snap. His aura is a deep ocean blue of contentment. I don't know what it says about me that I feel a shiver of satisfaction knowing I am partially responsible. It won't last—contentment never does. But it's there right now, and that feels like it means something.

I just don't know what.

Bram keeps speaking, oblivious to my strange thoughts. "Which is why I made a bargain with you the first night. You won't be able to help yourself; the pull of the answers is too strong for you to ignore." He gives me a long look. "But you weren't thinking about answers last night."

No, I really wasn't. All I was thinking about was where he would touch me next, kiss me next. Even now, with him standing a safe distance away, I'm achingly aware of the fact that I'm naked in his bed. It would be so easy to . . .

Damn it, I'm getting distracted again. It's one thing when I can convince myself I have no choice, but I can't quite make the leap into doing this now in the light of day. With that in mind, I slip out of the bed, ensuring I keep a careful distance between us as I head for the door. One of the downfalls of never being in a proper relationship is that I don't know how to navigate fighting in any way that resembles healthy. I'm so conflicted right now, I don't know which way is up, so it's better to get out of here before I say something I regret. "I'm going to take a walk." Maybe at the end of it, I'll have clarity.

"I never pegged you for a coward."

That stops me in my tracks. "I'm not a coward." You can't be in my line of work. Fear is death. Fear will make you freeze when you should run, run when you should fight. Fear will make you start screaming and lead the monsters right to your door. I've spent my entire life eradicating fear from the bottom of my bones and to my very soul. "Conducting a tactful retreat is intelligent."

"I see. We're still at war." He sounds so tired and defeated that I almost turn around. Almost. That way lies ruin. I have faltered already in so many ways. A week ago, the idea that I'd be worried about caring too much about my gargoyle would have made me laugh. Now, that threat is all too real.

I don't want to hurt him. But I can't afford to be distracted by him either.

I force my spine straight and shoulders back as I walk through the door without looking at him. He doesn't follow. I tell myself that's what I want as my footsteps echo through the empty hallways. How does he stand it? My own family home lies equally echoing and empty—I know that none of my late family members have made the transition to spirits—and I still take great pains not to spend more time there than necessary. The loneliness sinks in too quickly and takes root until I have to leave and rip it out of my soul with my bare hands.

Bram seems to embody the actual stone gargoyles that haunt the eaves of old churches and buildings. Hunched over against the elements, watching from above and isolated. I never felt sorry for those statues. I shouldn't feel sorry for him. He's choosing to stay here.

He is . . .

I stop short as a gargoyle steps into the hallway in front

of me. They're built short and robust with a barrel stomach and thighs that look like they could crush boulders. Like the other gargoyles I've glimpsed in the distance since I've come here, their only nod to modesty is a wrap around their hips. Gargoyles don't have the same hang-ups about chests that humans do. It makes sense when one accounts for how challenging it must be to create clothes that accommodate wings.

They don't say anything, which has the hairs on the back of my neck rising. "Can I help you?"

They study me for a bit too long. "I'm Luna. Their Noble Highness. My family line dates back to the founding of this territory."

I wait, but they don't say anything further. "Congratulations?"

They sigh like I've disappointed them. "You seem different than the humans I've met in the past. I'm hoping so, because I'd like to give you a piece of advice." They shift their wings in a way that I'm not sure how to decipher. Is it supposed to be comforting or threatening? I don't know enough about gargoyles to say for certain. "Bram and his family are cursed. He's not the last of his family line because of a series of unfortunate turns. Anyone who gets close to that family will die horribly. I highly suggest you put some distance between the two of you. And don't have his child."

Their tone seems honest enough, and their energy reflects nothing but sincerity. I know better than to trust that, though. If they're really one of the nobles, they likely learned to lie in the cradle. Learned to hide their energy from the time they were a child. I don't trust Bram, but I certainly don't trust a stranger. "Why would you warn me? You don't know me."

"Like I said, you don't seem to be a monster. Everyone

knows that you're trying to escape. That pendant around your neck is a good start, but it's all too easy to remove. If you have a child with him, the child will die. No one deserves to experience that loss."

A chill slides down my spine. "Are you threatening me and this theoretical child?" I have no intention of getting pregnant, but that doesn't stop the strange surge of protectiveness that I feel in response to their words.

"What? No!" To their credit, they sound genuinely horrified at the thought. "To do violence against an heir to the territory is unthinkable. The curse would pass to my family line and kill everyone I care about. I only meant to offer my assistance."

"Assistance," I echo.

They nod, some of the tension leaching from their shoulders. "Yes, exactly. As I said, your attempts at escape have been noted by those who witnessed them. We would like to offer assistance. One of us can take you wherever you want to go."

I refuse to feel humiliation over the fact that people aside from Bram witnessed my pathetic escape attempts. But I'm ridiculously embarrassed it never even occurred to me that others might see. I've barely seen anyone at all in my time in the castle, and fool that I am, I actually let myself believe it meant we were practically alone. I won't make that mistake again.

I can't trust this gargoyle. Right now, my presence here is the only thing that might provide Bram with an heir and displace any of the ambitious noble families who think they have a chance at leadership. They wouldn't even have to actively murder me. All it would take is a slip while flying high, and gravity would do the rest.

More than that, accepting help feels like cheating. If I'm going to escape, I'll do it on my own.

"While I appreciate the offer, I think you must understand why I can't accept it."

Luna shakes their head in disappointment. "You're making a mistake, but the offer stands. If you change your mind, you can find me in the east wing on the top floor."

I stand there and watch them walk away, then wait several more minutes to ensure I'm alone. I knew the situation was thorny, but I'm beginning to realize just how tangled things could get. Again, I wonder at my reluctance to leave the entire thing behind. I've been offered outs several times now, and every time, I resist. It doesn't make any sense.

Nothing about this place makes any sense.

I know better than to let my anger drive me, but I have too many fucking emotions right now. Anger is the easiest. And I know just who to bring it to.

17

BRAM

I hear her coming before I see her. I'd like to say the tread of Grace's feet is familiar to me already, but the truth is that no one else would bother to seek me out. I barely have a chance to look up when she charges into my office.

Grace huffs out a breath. "I've been looking for you everywhere."

"I've been here the whole time."

She's changed since leaving my bedroom this morning. Now she wears a pair of breeches that don't quite fit properly under a long tunic. Her long dark hair is free around her shoulders, and she should look young and ridiculous in her ill-fitting clothes. But I don't think Grace has ever looked young or ridiculous in her entire life. Not even when she was small and fundamentally helpless. The thought of her as a child leads to the thought of what her children might look like, which brings me a strange sort of sadness.

I want children. I don't know if I want them for the right reasons, but surely it isn't a bad thing to desire a family again. I know new family won't replace the siblings and father I lost, but maybe having someone to care for would leave me feeling less unmoored.

"This is fucking ridiculous, Bram. This has to end." Grace slams the door behind her. Her energy is a riot of red and the violet of resolve.

"It would help if I knew what you were angry about."

She paces from one side of my office to the other, her long strides eating up the distance, her fury almost wondrous to behold. "You are a laughingstock of a ruler."

That brings me up short. Of all the things I expected her to rage over, my abilities as a leader did not make the list. "Excuse me?"

"Your people respect you so little that they are actively undermining you right to my face. They know what I'm here for, and they don't care. They're not afraid that I'll come to you with the information, because they know you won't do anything about it."

Ah. "I see you've met one of the nobles. Who finally approached you?"

She pivots slowly to face me. The lack of momentum should make her less fearsome, but instead she feels like a predator that has narrowed their attention on me. "You knew this would happen?" she finally says.

"I knew it was a distinct possibility." I can't imagine the nobles have much faith in my ability to complete my goals, but most of them aren't complete fools. They know what's at stake if I succeed. It was only a matter time before one of them approached her. There are few foolish enough to threaten her, and none of those people are currently in residence. I would like to pretend it's me—or the curse—they fear, but the truth is that no one wants to cross Azazel. He's proven himself to be a fearsome warrior, and he's intensely protective of his humans. Years ago, one of the incubi violated his hospitality and harmed one of his humans. He made such an example of her that I suspect any of us who saw the results have that scene imprinted in our nightmares.

And he ensured that all of us saw.

Grace is still looking at me like I have sprouted an additional set of horns. "And you're . . . okay with this?"

Her frustration is so thick, I can almost feel the friction of it against my skin. "Of course I'm not okay with it. They obviously upset you, and that's not something I want for you ever."

"Upset me." She says the words with absolutely no inflection. "Is that what you think this is?"

"I can see that it is." I wave my hand to encompass her energy, which is swirling about the room and filling the space.

I realize I made a mistake the second she goes perfectly still. "Your people are actively plotting against you. Do you know what they offered me? An escape from this place. I might not have taken them up on it this time, but enough rejections and they're going to realize that I won't ever. What happens then, Bram? I'll tell you what happens. They escalate. I don't know what circumstances would be enough for them to believe there's a real chance you might convince me to have a child, but they won't allow it. Not when their goals are so close at hand. And all you have to say is that you don't want me *upset*?"

I know better than to let my anger slip its leash. And yet her derision pricks at me. "What do you want me to do?"

"Literally anything!"

Tension coils through me, but I force myself to sit back slowly instead of surging to my feet. "There's nothing to be done. They believe I'm cursed, and so they won't listen to me. Until I can prove otherwise, we're in a holding pattern."

"That is the biggest load of shit I've ever heard." She points a finger at me. "You're just going through the motions. You don't want this. You don't want any of this. Gods, you're probably waiting for someone to come along and stab you in the back and put you out of your misery."

The truth of her words stings worse than anything she could do to me physically. That, more than anything else she's said since entering my office, provokes me to action. I rise and flare out my wings. "Get out."

"Or what?" She lifts her brows and sneers. "Are you going to muscle me out? Please. You're more likely to go to your knees and offer me your throat. Just like I imagine you do in any important conversation that comes into your life these days. At least I have no intention of cutting it. I can't say the same for the rest of the people in this castle."

"Get. Out."

For a long moment, I think she'll press the issue. But she lowers her hand and shakes her head slowly. "You're not doing yourself any favors with this half life, Bram. I'll see you at dinner." She turns and stalks out of the room.

If only her words left with her.

They plague me through the afternoon. There's not much work to be done, which means there aren't many distractions to be had. The territory more or less runs itself. It has since before my father's time. The only real purpose that the leader has is to ensure the different gargoyle factions remain of equal power and to lead us during wartime. The former is a full-time job, or at least it was before the different noble families mostly withdrew from this castle. Now I don't know what they're doing at all. The spies my father had have all melted away in the night. I am well and truly alone.

I'm doing the best I fucking can, and I deeply resent

Grace for acting as if I'm not. Who is she to talk? She's got plenty of her own skeletons rattling around in that impressive closet inside her.

By the time the sun sets and I make my way down to the kitchen to check on dinner, I am so furious, I can barely speak. Silas gives me a strange look the moment I walk through the door. "Big plans tonight?"

"What makes you say that?" I'm being too brusque, but I can't stop myself. There's a part of me that's jealous that he already saw her; there's no other reason for him to be asking that question. "Where is she?"

He raises his brows. "Maybe it would be better if you ate separately tonight."

Part of me wonders if he's right, but the rest of me can't stand the thought of keeping all this tumultuous energy inside me with no outlet. Grace will be fine. She always is. "We'll eat like normal."

"If you insist." Silas turns back to the stove.

I am taking out many years of frustration and fear on the convenient target that is Grace. I can't bring myself to give a fuck. Somehow, everything comes to a point when I see the formal dining room. Place after place set out in perfect symmetry. All empty. Just like normal.

Except for one.

Grace sits right in the center of the long length, dressed in a black gown. This one seems to fit her better than the others, at least the part I can see. It clings to her arms and breasts, leaving her shoulders and most of her upper chest bare. She's fastened her hair up into some intricate style that looks lovely. She's even colored her lips, a deep crimson shade that makes me think of blood.

Taunting me in my office wasn't enough. She's going to drive the point home with the ferocity of a warrior out for their enemy's death. I want to hate her for it, but I can't help admiring her willingness to step onto the field of battle.

I don't walk to the head of the table. Instead, I take the seat directly across from her. We stare at each other as the minutes tick by. I know that to speak first is to lose, but at some point, this is just ridiculous. "Congratulations, you've proven your point."

"Have I?" She leans back and spreads her arms. "Where are your people, Bram? Do they respect you so little that they don't worry about their absence here? Don't bother to answer. I already know."

My earlier frustration and anger bubbles right out of my mouth before I can think better of it. "That's rich coming from you. You act like you know so much about responsibility and taking care of your own. Yet the first chance you got, you abandoned your entire realm and came into this one to find answers about a dead woman. What the fuck does it matter how she died, Grace? It doesn't change anything. It certainly doesn't take away from the fact that you're running from your problems, same as me. I think that's what pisses you off the most about me. We. Are. The. Same."

"The *fuck* we are."

Now it's my turn to lean back, to smirk at her as she unravels the same way I did earlier in my office. This is childish. But I want to be under her skin and just as aggravating as she is to me. That satisfaction is empty, but I don't care. I press forward well beyond any good sense. "You're so angry, Grace. Do you think I'm not? But then, the most aggravating thing in the world is to look at another person and see your perfect mirror. Changing me won't change how you feel. It won't change *you*."

She plants her hands on the table and rises abruptly. "Shut the fuck up."

"Or what?" I see the answer in her energy—little pops of the threat of violence. Now is the time to turn us back to safety. I won't. This is the moment I tuck my wings close to my body and let gravity take hold. The moment I embrace it, throw myself against the most basic law of existing: what goes up must come down. And when it does, it hurts like nothing else.

This moment with Grace is ugly and awful, but at least it's real. If I make her angry enough to kill me? That's something she'll have to live with. Not me.

"Or maybe we'll find out if you really do burn after all." She's practically shaking with fury. It's a beautiful sight, though I don't know what it says about me that I think so.

I don't burn. I don't feel much temperature fluctuation at all, courtesy of my skin. I won't say that Grace is no danger to me, but I recognize that she's taking an avenue that will cause no permanent damage and might make us both feel better. I doubt she's doing it intentionally . . . but I am. It's toxic, but I don't give a fuck.

"Silas." I barely have to raise my voice. I know he's standing just out of sight around the doorway to the kitchen. I can sense him there, his curiosity and worry lingering at the edge of my line of sight.

He emerges a few seconds later, and I can appreciate that he doesn't appear like he was eavesdropping. "Are you ready to eat?"

"I think we'll skip straight to dessert. Please bring me matches, oil, and those lovely little marshmallow things you made earlier today." They're soft and gooey and should burn rather nicely.

To his credit, Silas doesn't hesitate, though I catch more

worry in his energy before he slips away. There's no worry in *Grace* as I turn back to her. She has her eyes narrowed in suspicion. "What are you up to?"

"One of the first times you ever spoke to me was to ask if I burn. Let's find out together." I lean forward, bracing my elbows on the table, daring her with my eyes to back down. "You might like the way I fuck, but don't pretend you like me. Don't pretend you don't crave freedom from my presence to pursue your poor, dead mother. So burn me, Grace. Unless you don't really want answers at all. Maybe you're just as much a coward as I am. I'm your mirror, after all."

18

GRACE

This godsdamned fool of a gargoyle. After the shit show in his office this afternoon, I realized he didn't understand. I don't have the words to make him. I don't have the time. I sure as fuck don't have the patience.

But then he comes here and throws my vulnerability back in my face? I didn't have to let him in, even the smallest amount, yesterday. I might not have given him the full truth, but I didn't have to confess even that much. Now I'm glad he doesn't know everything about me and my family. If *this* is how he returns vulnerability, best not to show it at all.

And now he wants to use me to hurt himself.

Neither of us speaks as Silas comes back into the room with a small tray. He hesitates for a moment and then sets it on the center of the table between us. It contains an artful display of matches in a round container, a little gravy boat thing that appears to have oil in it, and a pyramid of fluffy square marshmallows. He walks out of the room without another word.

I'd like to believe this is a bluff, but I know Bram well

enough now to recognize his lack of hesitation. The problem is that the man has no self-preservation. Which might mean that he'll be fine if I follow through on this ridiculously risky path . . . Or it might mean that he's about to die right in front of me. My fury burns hotter at the acknowledgment. He calls me selfish, but what is this? I don't expect him to genuinely care for me—at least I don't think I do—but this is so cruel, I can barely stand it. I should walk away. In fact, I will walk away. Right fucking now.

Except I don't.

I sit my ass back down in the chair and reach over to take the container of matches. I hold Bram's eyes as I sit back and place a single match, head down, between my middle finger and the table. It's a stone table, so it'll work just as well as a matchbox. I strike the match and flick it toward him. It lights and sails through the air toward Bram. It lands on his plate and sizzles for a moment before burning itself out.

"Cute bluff. But I don't think you have the courage to do it for real." He grabs the container of oil and pours it over his chest. Even knowing I should look away, I can't help tracing the path the oil takes down his chest to his waist. I know how those muscles feel beneath my hands, my tongue, pressed against my breasts and back.

I know better than to let my rage take the wheel. Nothing good comes from losing control. Only pain.

I reach for another match. We're playing a game of chicken that might have deadly consequences. This is toxic and a huge indicator that we are a terrible pair. Neither one of us has the brakes to divert this runaway train. I can't stand the thought of him calling me a coward again. More, a dark part of me wants to punish him, to prove that he doesn't actually want to die.

I flick another match toward him. This one lands on a napkin next to the plate, and we both watch in silence as it goes up in flames. Bram looks at me, and all the tension leaches out of his body. He gives me a cocky smile. "Surely you can do better than that. If not, we're going to be here all night."

I am a broken creature. I've known that about myself for as long as I've been aware enough to understand that my family is not like other families. If I had any kindness, any self-preservation, it was trained out of me before I knew the meaning of the word. Normal people don't fall back on violence as the first solution to any problem. Normal people lose sleep at night when they end a life, justified or not. Normal people . . . But then, I'm not normal. I never have been.

I flick a third match toward him.

This one lands right in his lap. I watch in horror as the flames course up his chest. I belatedly realize I'm on my feet without having had any intention of standing, my hand closing around my goblet of water, when the rest of what I'm seeing registers.

Bram hasn't moved. He hasn't flinched. He's not writhing in pain or screaming. He's just sitting there staring at me with that self-satisfied smirk on his face. Apparently gargoyles really don't burn. I get a flash of his teeth through the flames. "Do you feel better now?"

"Hardly. I was merely indulging in this stunt of yours." I grab a marshmallow and shove it onto a long fork. I perch a hip on the table and lean over so I can reach the heat coming off the flames on his body. Are my hands shaking? I can't tell. The entirety of me seems to be racked with tremors. Not my voice, though. I sound remarkably normal when I speak. "Do *you* feel better? Does this change anything at all?"

Bram, the bastard, laughs as the flames slowly dwindle away to nothing.

It snaps something inside me. I crawl across the table and shove the marshmallow into his mouth. He makes a surprised noise. He isn't laughing anymore. He starts to spit it out, but I grip his jaw closed. I'm not touching him anywhere else, so all he has to do is lean back to escape my grasp. "What's wrong, Bram? Don't you like the taste of your own consequences?"

He holds my gaze as he chews slowly. It can't be entirely comfortable with me holding his jaw, but Bram seems to crave the discomfort I give him. When he swallows, I shift my grip to his cheeks and pinch hard. It forces his mouth open a little, and he makes a sound that has nothing to do with pain.

I'm so angry, I can barely see straight. One thing I always prided myself on was that I never let my violence take control. Not unless the situation called for it and there was no other option. I can't say that's the truth tonight. There were plenty of other options that didn't include me flicking match after match at his oiled-up body. I wondered if he was using me to hurt himself and even that wasn't enough to make me stop.

I study his face, the way his brows have relaxed now that he views me as being in control. "It's not fair, you know." I pinch him a little harder, earning yet another sexy whimper. "You're being an asshole to provoke a reaction out of me to make yourself feel better. If you want me to punish you, all you have to do is ask. But this? This shit is unhealthy, and if you do it again, I'm walking away for good. Do you understand me?"

He tries to speak, but I don't release him. Finally, Bram nods slowly. I'm nearly certain that he's only agreeing to appease me, but I don't care. His energy is a swirly mass of colors that makes me dizzy to look at. I've never felt more like a monster than I do right now. I release him and push his face away. It's awkward climbing down from the table, but it's a small price to pay for escaping this room and situation.

I lit him on fire.

Of all the unhinged, unacceptable courses of action, that has to top the list. That's something my grandfather would've done. It's not something you do to someone you care about.

The realization that I care about him is almost enough to give me pause, but my need to escape is stronger. I don't run for the door, but I move with urgency. I almost make it, too.

"Grace." Bram doesn't lift his voice, but it feels like he reaches across the room and hooks me in the chest. I stop. Even as I tell myself not to, I turn to face him once more. He's exactly where I left him. The only change is that his wings now droop on the ground, mirroring the defeated slope of his shoulders. "I'm sorry. I took it too far."

"We both did." I flee from the room.

I SPEND the next week avoiding Bram and every other gargoyle who tries to cross my path. This happens with increasing frequency as I keep myself busy exploring the castle. I don't see Luna again, but the other nobles have obviously taken a page from their book and want to approach me too. I have no interest in that bullshit.

The fact that I can see auras helps. All I need is a glimpse of color to know I need to change my route. Day after day passes, and Bram doesn't seek me out. I'm pretty sure he's following me, shadowing my path through the winding halls and spiraling staircases, but he's a much subtler hunter than his people are. The only indication I have that he's there at all is a hot feeling at the back of my neck.

I don't know if he's being a coward or if I am. Probably both. I scared myself that night in the dining room. Worst of all, I'm pretty sure he only apologized because I was upset, not because he felt like things were out of control. Bram has no brakes. And I don't when I'm with him either. It's a recipe for disaster.

The clearest answer is the one I refuse to accept. I should leave. I haven't seen Ramanu since that first visit, but I've taken to carrying around the ring they gave me in my pocket. All I have to do is speak their name to summon them, and they will whisk me away to bargainer territory once more. The thought should fill me with relief, but instead it makes me want to dig in my heels all the more.

I find the massive cave on the seventh day. It's so wide that I can't see the far walls as I carefully descend the staircase. Down and down and down, so deep that I'm surprised I can't feel the pressure against my skin. Gargoyles might be people of the sky, but there's plenty of space to fly here in this room. Once I reach the bottom, I am surprised to find buildings carved into the stone. It's an . . . underground city?

I only explore a little bit before caution gets the best of me and I ascend once more to return to my room. But curiosity is a powerful thing, and the next day I'm back in the depths, exploring the streets between the strange stone buildings. There's no sign of life, no food or perishables. But there is furniture, and I notice a distinct lack of dust in the few places I dare explore.

What *is* this place?

On the third day of exploring it, I enter far enough into the city—because it *is* a city—to find the underground river. Curiosity causes me to dip my fingers into the icy water and press them to my lips. The water's fresh. Possibly even drinkable.

"Back away from the water, Grace."

I startle so badly, I almost fall into the river. I didn't hear Bram approaching. I didn't even feel his attention on me this time either. Apparently I don't move fast enough, because he lands next to me and hauls me back ten feet. He releases me just as quickly as he grabbed me, doing a strange hop that, accompanied by the flap of his wings, sends him farther away. "I'm sorry. But it's not safe. That river goes all the way to the sea, and the kraken people can reach this place using it."

"I thought you weren't at war." It's such a silly thing to say. Only my shock excuses the ridiculousness of it.

"Just because we're not at war doesn't mean you're not in danger. Plenty of accidents happen during peacetime." He looks around us. "Why do you keep coming back here?"

That's the question, isn't it? There are other things I should be doing. If I really mean to escape . . . But I can't lie to myself and say that's the goal anymore. If it were, I would have made it work by now. I don't even have to go through the dramatics of escaping when all I have to do is summon Ramanu. If I haven't done that by now, I'm not going to.

The realization washes over me, bringing something

almost like relief. I don't want to leave. Bram and I've been absolute disasters for each other, but I'm drawn to him like I've never been drawn to another person before. He might not know my full history, or be able to map every scar, but he sees my fault lines clearly enough. Anyone else would look away, would *turn* away.

Not Bram.

He was right before. In some ways, looking at him is like looking into a fractured mirror. I don't know what it says about me that I want to touch him so much, I'm willing to cut myself on the mirrored pieces.

"I think the more important question is: Why are you following me?"

19

BRAM

I told myself I was protecting Grace by following her. The truth is that I can't stand the thought of having more distance between us than necessary. It seems like I haven't done anything except fuck up since meeting her, but she hasn't taken her readily available exit route. Azazel would remove her from my presence without a second thought if she asked. She hasn't asked. I want to believe that means something. I'm terrified that it doesn't.

I owe her honesty. Truth be told, I owe her a whole lot more than that. "You were right before. I wanted to provoke a response out of you, and I didn't care if you were hurt by it. I didn't care if I was hurt by it, either."

"I know."

The tailor I finally convinced to come to the castle has done good work with Grace's clothing. She wears fitted pants, sturdy boots, and a thick tunic that seems to be keeping away the cold of this cave.

Even so, I can't help being worried about her. I shouldn't have been surprised that she ended up in the part of the castle that houses so many ghosts. Not literal ones, at least not that I'm aware of. But the history of my people and their sorrow is written in stone here. This place was only built because of the war. It never would've existed if not for the death and destruction that came to the keep. Gargoyles will not willingly be cut off from the sky unless there's no other option.

"This location is kept in case of emergency. It's large enough to house the full population of this castle at capacity, and then some. The river is the only weakness, but fresh water is worth the risk. If you move north from here, there's a bridge that will take you across the river to the gardens. They're tended at all times, even now. Most of our food in the castle comes from there because it's important to keep them functioning, and wasting food is unacceptable. Anything extra goes to neighboring villages." There's plenty of extra these days. Feeding a handful of people in residence barely makes a dent in the garden's bounty. "Deeper into the mountains, there are a number of local creatures who can be hunted to supplement stores and ensure no one goes without."

Instead of looking horrified, Grace just appears thoughtful. "It's honestly a brilliant bunker. How do you keep the garden growing so deep beneath the surface?"

"Magic. Certain stones can be spelled to mimic sunlight in every way." I motion at the ceiling overhead hidden in shadow. "There are several veins of that same stone running through these mountains. Plenty enough to keep my people stocked for generation—longer if they're careful."

"You've gated the openings of the underground river?"

"Yes. It's not a foolproof system. Should the kraken people want to gain entry, I'm sure they'd be able to, but we should hear them coming. Beyond that, there are guards posted to monitor the banks." Or at least there normally were. I've lost them as well in the past few years.

Thane is a good leader to the kraken people, though. He doesn't seek out confrontation if there is any other option available. More than that, I've managed to negotiate several lucrative trading deals with him that he is as invested in protecting as I am. There's plenty of danger in this realm, and I'm not naive enough to believe that trade deals will prevent war, but if there's immediate danger, I don't believe it comes from the krakens.

Grace tucks her hair behind her ears and gives me a long look. "You've been following me."

Shame heats my skin, and I'm grateful I don't flush the way humans do when they're embarrassed. "I don't like how we left things, but I didn't know how to approach you to fix them. I wasn't sure you wanted to see me."

"I didn't at first." She turns back toward the entrance and pauses until I realize she means for me to walk next to her. We tread in silence for several blocks. Finally, she says, "I would like to understand. We both have our secrets and plenty of trauma to go around, but if we continue like this, I don't think we'll last the year, let alone seven."

Something like hope takes root in my chest. It's such a foreign sensation that several beats go by before I understand what I'm feeling. "I thought you were bent on escape."

"I was." Sorrow colors her in pale blue. "You were right, even if you were cruel. Things back home haven't been the same since the last of my family died. I don't know if I believe in what we were doing anymore. I want to think I helped people. I'm *certain* I helped people. But at what cost? When someone like me makes a mistake, people die. And they're not always the ones who deserve it."

I want nothing more than to take her in my arms. I'm not

sure if she'll accept it, though. I suppose the only way to find out is to ask. "Grace." I wait for her to pause and turn to me. It takes more courage than I would've imagined to lift my arms in invitation.

She doesn't hesitate. She steps into my embrace and allows me to wrap her up tightly. It's the most natural thing in the world to enclose us in my wings. There, in the intimate darkness of my own making, I finally find the courage to tell her the truth. "The reason everyone in my territory believes I'm cursed is because I'm the only surviving member of the massacre that killed my entire family. And I'm only alive because I hid when they were attacked."

Grace tenses. "I know I said I want to know, but if it's going to hurt you, you don't have to tell me."

"I hurt all the time, Grace. What's a little more if it helps fix things between us?" I run my hand down her back, allowing her presence to comfort me. "It was my father's fault. He started spending time in the bargainer demon territory after the war, avoiding his duties as leader, and he got hooked on humans. I think Azazel was looking for any leverage he could find to ensure the peace talks succeeded. So he made a bargain with my father, very similar to the one I made." Almost identical, in fact. Not that it matters now. I take a slow breath, inhaling Grace's scent. "Less than a year in, she killed everyone. Even my siblings, who had barely entered adulthood."

"Bram," Grace breathes. "Saying I'm sorry is useless, but I truly am sorry for your loss. I know what it's like to have violence touch your family and leave a ragged hole of nothingness behind. I wouldn't wish that on my worst enemy, let alone someone I care about."

Someone she cares about.

I know better than to take her word at anything other

than face value. I knew before that she didn't hate me, or she would have escaped properly by now. But not hating is a long way from caring . . . or even love. Not that I expect love from Grace. I sure as fuck don't deserve it.

"He let his desire for humans override his responsibilities, and when that wasn't enough, he brought pain and death into our family because he wanted a human of his very own to possess." I drag in a breath. "His selfishness paved the way for our destruction. If this happened in any other territory, it would've been a tragedy beyond measure. Because it happened here, where my people like to attach deeper meaning to every action and word, they almost unilaterally decided that his actions and poor judgment brought a curse onto our family line. Some days, I even think it's the truth."

Grace hugs me tighter. "You're not cursed. You've just gone through something horrific. I know you won't believe me when I say this, but the fact that you lived doesn't make you a coward. It makes you a survivor. There's a whole lot of baggage and guilt that goes along with that, but the alternative is you being dead. I'll never say *that* is the preferable outcome."

Once again, shame coats me, so strong that I can barely breathe past it. "I don't know what I'm doing. I wasn't supposed to take this position of rulership for years and years. I don't even want it anymore. But there's no other option. If I step down, it will hurt my people."

She strokes her hands in a soothing movement along my sides. "You don't need to have all the answers right now. I don't think anyone expects that. You just have to take it one day at a time."

I don't ask her if she understands the gravity of what she is telling me to do. She does. Out of anyone, Grace understands taking it one day at a time means moving into the future instead of dwelling on the past. Which makes what I've done to her all the worse. "I shouldn't have pushed you the other night. I sure as fuck shouldn't have thrown your mother's death in your face. I'm sorry."

She gives a choked laugh. "It seems like we're always going to be apologizing to each other. You were right; in a way, we are reflections of each other. Which can be a great comfort, but it also means we know exactly what to say or do to hurt the other. Something to keep in mind for the future." She gives me one last squeeze. "My entire family is dead, too. They didn't go out together, and not every one of the deaths was violent, but they're gone all the same. I don't have a kingdom to rule, but my family has something of a legacy that I'm supposed to fulfill. That my . . . children . . . are supposed to continue to fulfill. Maybe that should give me purpose, but the only thing I feel is exhaustion. I'm so damned tired of fighting."

"What if . . ." I speak slowly, feeling my way. "What if instead of fighting, we started to build something?" She tenses slightly, and I realize I'm not communicating properly. "I don't mean a family. I won't pretend that I don't want that, just like I won't pretend that the idea of starting one with *you* isn't attractive in a way I was never prepared to experience. But it's been a couple of weeks. It's too soon to make that jump."

"A week and a half ago, you were raring and ready to put a baby in my belly."

As much as I want to keep holding her, I think it's best we're able to see each other properly for this conversation. I slowly take a step back. Grace's eyes shine in the shadows of the cave, and her energy is a thick gray of worry, but otherwise she looks okay.

"Ultimately, I don't think a child will fix my current problems." It's such a relief to say that out loud, I let loose a breathless laugh. "A child won't fix my problems."

She's staring at me strangely. "You made a demon deal for the possibility of a child, and you were so desperate for it that you were willing to gamble your kingdom."

"Yes. I was. But things change." I beat my wings slowly, reveling in this new lack of burden. Rationally, I know it's not actually physical, but it feels that way. "I know that I can be stubborn and infuriating, but I *do* listen when you speak. You've been thinking for the last week and a half while you wandered the castle. I have, too. If I don't fix things as they are now, all I'm going to be doing is passing along my burdens to any children I have." The enormity of what will be required threatens to prick my good mood, but I set that aside for now. There will be plenty of time to stress about anything and everything later.

Grace crosses her arms over her chest. A little light green feathers through the gray of her worry. I've got her. Once her curiosity takes hold, she won't stop until she has answers. "I suspect you're right. But I'm going to need you to tell me a whole lot more about this change."

"It's time to fix things. Or at least start to fix things." I hold out my arms. "Would you like to come with me?"

"Where we going?" Grace takes a cautious step toward me.

I swing her up into my arms and launch into the air. "We're going to call the council."

20

GRACE

From how dramatic his declaration was, I half expected Bram to somehow summon his people with magic. In reality, it turns out that calling the council involves a whole lot of paperwork. There's not much I can do to help, but he seems to find my presence supportive, so I perch on the edge of his desk and watch him write up several summons.

"What if they don't come?"

"They will." He finishes a letter and waits for the ink to dry before he carefully folds it up and seals it with wax. "If they don't, I will strip them of their land and titles."

I blink. "You can do that?"

"Technically, yes. It hasn't been done in generations, but I need them to take me seriously. As much as I don't relish using their fear against them, it's necessary to ensure they obey."

I watch him draft another letter in silence. For the short time I've known him, Bram has very intentionally gone out of his way not to make waves. The only time he's really dug in his heels with me was when he caught me sneaking out that first time. Watching him now, seeing the stubborn set of his brow and the determination in his movements, I can't help the feeling that sinks its roots into my very core. It's warm and comforting and yet terrifying all the same.

"You don't need my approval, but I'm proud of you. I know this isn't easy for you."

He pauses, then speaks without looking up at me. "I might not need your approval, but I appreciate it all the same." Bram finishes this letter and goes through the same process of drying and sealing it. "My father was a good leader when he first took the position. Or at least that's what everyone says. I don't know if it's true. Long as I can remember, he avoided his duties, seeking his pleasure over the benefit of our people. I've found that when a person dies, people have a habit of washing away their sins."

"I've found the same." IMy legs are tired from all the stairs this past week. A few weeks ago, I could have done them without blinking, but I haven't kept up with my training. I didn't realize until now that it's been a relief to let go of it. I *like* being active, but I've always had an ulterior motive. Weakness is something an enemy will exploit. If I'm not good enough, I will die and possibly get others killed as well. That pressure really takes any enjoyment out of training.

I take a slow breath and refocus on the present . . . more or less. The past never seems to be far when I'm with Bram. I still don't know if that's a good thing or a bad thing. "When my grandfather died, it was like the moment he passed, he took all the unforgivable shit with him. I barely recognized the man my family talked about in the aftermath. It didn't make sense to me then, and it doesn't make sense to me now. The pain people cause by being horrible and selfish and monstrous doesn't magically disappear with them."

"No. It doesn't." Bram sits back and holds out a hand. "Come here."

I've never been one for cuddling and the like, but it seems that a lot of things I thought were true don't hold up with this man. It's the most natural thing in the world to take his hand and allow him to tug me down onto his lap and wrap his arms around me. I rest my head on his shoulder and allow the warmth of his skin to soothe me. "How do we move forward? Some days it feels like I'm drowning in the past and everything I've lost. I know what my family would want from me, but I'm so tired of fighting. I don't want to do it anymore. I just . . . I don't know who I am if I'm not what they created me to be." It's the first time I've spoken the words aloud. The truth of the sentence is so stark that it feels like I've reached into the very heart of me.

"You don't have to decide now." Bram runs his hand over my hair and down my back. "No matter what else is true, you have time. Whatever you decide will be the right choice."

"Just like that?"

"Yes." He kisses my temple. "You're strong, you're smart, and you're driven. I have no doubt that you'll conquer whatever you set your mind to, regardless of the arena."

His confidence warms me just as much as his comfort. He believes it. I don't have to check his aura to know it to be true. I press my hand to his chest, right over the steady thump of his heart. Would he have such confidence in me if he knew the truth of my past, my family? I might toe the line of being a true monster, but many in my family have crossed right over it happily.

I don't believe that the sins of the people in your life bleed into you . . . normally.

He's given me so much truth, so much vulnerability.

Maybe I can return the favor without it blowing up in my face. I close my eyes and take what I hope is a fortifying breath. "When the realms separated, there were people and . . . things stranded in realms that weren't their home."

"I know the histories," he says carefully.

"I don't know what happened in the other realms, but humans have always been at the bottom of the food chain. We can breed with paranormals and gift our children powers, but if we don't survive long enough to bear that child, to see them grow to adulthood . . . Well, either way, it doesn't help the parent any."

Bram has gone so still, he might as well have become stone like the gargoyles that haunt the dark high places of so many buildings. "Yes."

"To some of the monsters left behind, it was the equivalent of an all-you-can-eat buffet. Most of the human population isn't even aware paranormals exist or that monsters are real, which only makes them easier prey. Several families decided to do something about it. Mine was one of them." I don't know why this is so hard to say. Maybe because most of my family would consider Bram a monster to be exterminated on sight. "They—we—saved a lot of people over the generations, but . . . Gods, Bram, it's no way to live. One of my first memories is of my father handing me a knife and drilling me on where to stab a body to ensure they bleed out before they can hurt me."

His arms tighten around me, just a little. "I'm sorry."

"Don't be. I'm still alive. No one else is." My breath shudders out. "But I'm the last one left. To continue the family legacy would mean having kids for the sole purpose of turning them into hunters. Of breaking them before the world can so they will be the most efficient killers possible. I . . . I can't do it. I don't *want* to do it. I think I want kids, but

I'm so afraid some switch inside me will flip and I'll turn into my parents. They loved me, but they hurt me and told me it would make me stronger."

"Strength isn't worth the cost of everything else," he says softly. "But you are not your parents. You're already making different choices than they did."

That's what's so scary. My map for life has gone up in flames, and every step I take, I'm worried the ground will give out beneath me. "I don't know how to be someone who isn't a hunter. I don't know how to deal with the toxic combination of guilt and relief that I feel when I think about leaving it all behind." There are other families, and other hunters, but it's always been drilled into my head that Jaegers were a cut above the rest. That no one else can compare.

"I don't know how to be someone who isn't cursed." He brushes another kiss to my temple.

All my training, all my experience, screams that this is a terrible decision. I came to the demon realm with one purpose and one purpose only. But, as much as I don't want to face it, Bram was right when he said that finding out the truth of my mother won't ultimately change anything. It won't bring her back. It won't make me feel less alone.

I lean back, and Bram lets me. There's nothing but open honesty on his face. His aura has a tentative thread of hope. He smiles briefly. "Why don't we find out who we are without the shadow of our parents . . . together?"

Together. "This is too fast. You don't know me. I don't know you." I'm grasping at straws, and yet, at the same time, these are perfectly reasonable statements.

"Maybe." He shrugs. "I don't know your favorite color. I don't know your parents' names or a number of relatively important details. But, Grace." He cups my face with one large hand. "I know *you*. I've known you from the first."

I lift my brows, instinctively striving to ease the moment. "The first?"

"Well, not the very first. But the moment you ran and then didn't flinch at the anger I brought, when you met me at the line I drew in the sand and forced me to do the same . . . I knew you then."

Part of me wants to push back against this knowing, to protect the inner soft parts of me that are far too easily bruised. No one has gotten as close as Bram, and he's right —it's not a matter of time. It's a soul-deep recognition that feels like magic yet is something much more mundane but no less a gift. We're two survivors, cast adrift in the choices those around us made. We can spend the rest of our lives being tossed to and fro in the waves of others' making . . .

Or we can choose a different path.

"I suppose that's how life works." I speak slowly, feeling my way. "It's filled with people making the best of each day, no matter what it brings."

Bram's smile warms. "That's what I hear."

"Are you done with the letters?"

"I just need to hand them off to be sent."

I ease off his lap and take a careful step away. "You should do that. Right now." I trail my hand over my collarbone and keep moving back. "In a hurry."

His pale eyes heat. "What will you be doing in the meantime?"

"Waiting naked in your bed." It's so incredibly gratifying to see his wings flare. With time, I think I'll get as good at reading his body language as I am at reading his aura. I smile. "I have my bargain to fulfill, after all. I promised that you could have me any way you want me."

"You did, didn't you?" He hasn't moved, but he watches me so closely, I have the feeling he could cross the room in a single bound and pin me to the wall. If I tell him to chase me, he will. I'm sure of it.

Another time.

"Yes," I finally manage.

He nods. "What I want is just *us*. No games. No power plays. Just you and I."

Somehow that's scarier than anything we've done so far. Except that's not entirely true. We just cut open our chests and showed each other our bleeding centers. Having sex without any scaffolding isn't much different than that. I lick my lips. "Okay."

"I'll see you shortly."

I back slowly out the door and head through the halls to the staircase that will lead me to Bram's room. I'm cautious. It's not that this situation feels too good to be true—it's far too messy for that—but this is the first time in my life that I've allowed myself to be fully vulnerable with another person. I can't help waiting for the other shoe to drop and take me out in the process.

No. I'm not doing that. I've spent my entire life being vigilant and keeping people at a distance. I can afford to change that this once, to allow Bram close. It might not be an easy path, but with him I might have a chance at true happiness . . .

21

BRAM

I find Grace exactly as promised—naked in my bed.

It's a sight I'll never get used to. She isn't doing anything particularly provocative, just sitting with the sheets pooled around her waist and her breasts exposed, her dark hair pushed back from her face. But she's in *my* bed. Naked and vulnerable and trusting.

I shut the door behind me and drink in the image she presents. "I like you like this."

"I'm naked. Of course you like me like this." She laughs a little, but color rises in her pale cheeks.

This feels like a big step that I'm not entirely certain we've earned, but that's not going to stop me. What's the point of time when in some ways I feel like I've known this woman my entire life? I can't stop myself from holding my breath.

"Are you sure you want it like this? Just me. No games."

"Yes. Is this okay with you?" No matter what the bargain between me and Grace says, I don't want to push her into anything she doesn't want to do. I never have, even when anger was riding me hard. I still don't know how to put into words what I feel for Grace. But maybe I can show her. Not with colors or energy or magic. With my touch. Sometimes it's better to say less, especially when my words so often get away from me.

She finally nods. "Yes, Bram. Of course it's okay with me. It's not like you're asking to fuck me while we're flying."

My body surges hot, but I shut the thought down quickly. "That's not a good idea. Even without the temperature at play, it'd be too easy to hurt you."

I can practically see her interest sharpening. "But it can be done?"

"In theory. It's not something my people do or at least admit to doing. It's incredibly dangerous, especially when both parties have wings." It would be too easy to get tangled and not be able to pull out of a dive. When I was a teenager, it was common to talk about the semantics and if it was even possible. I know several people that swore it was and went further to say they would prove it. To the best of my knowledge, none of them ever tried.

None of that information matters now.

I undo my hip wrap and toss it to the side. It's not a move I make to shut off this topic of conversation, but it's effective nonetheless. Grace's eyes fall to my hips, and hot pink lights the room up. She licks her lips. "Again, to reiterate, I am very, very okay with this. Come to bed."

She doesn't have to tell me twice. I cross to the bed and climb onto it. I don't have a plan. I just need to touch her, to kiss her. Apparently she feels exactly the same because she meets me in the middle. Our height difference means it's challenging to kiss when we're both on our knees, but I solve the problem by grabbing her around the hips and lifting her so she can wrap her legs around my waist. Better. Much better.

We don't have anywhere else to be right now. There's no rush, no ticking clock. I can kiss her as long as I like. And so I do. I hold her aloft and tease her mouth open. She digs her fingers into my hair but makes no move to take control. We're too busy clinging to each other and enjoying the moment.

Every moment with this woman is larger than life, and this one is no different. She consumes me. I can't get enough of her taste, of the feel of her skin sliding against mine, of the desperate little noises she makes that are both demands and pleas. I wrap my wings around us without a conscious thought. I just need more. I need to feel her.

I shift my grip without dislodging her, moving one hand to cup her ass so I can press a finger into her pussy. She's soaked. Even better, she breaks the kiss to press her forehead hard against mine. Her exhales ghost frantically against my lips. "That feels really good."

"It feels really good to me, too." I pump slowly, achingly aware of the fact that I have to ready her for my cock. "You're so damned hot and wet, gripping my finger like a vise. It makes me wild."

I wedge a second finger into her. Grace's thighs tense as she tries to lift herself and ride my fingers, but the angle isn't good for it. "Bram, please!"

"I'm not playing games. I'm not going to make you wait." The feeling of her around my fingers is almost enough to make me come on the spot. I want this. I love knowing she's wet and needy and demanding for me and what I can give her. I love that she doesn't hesitate to communicate what she wants. "But I won't lie and pretend this doesn't get me even harder, Grace. You can't rush me in this position. I can hold you like this until the end of time, making you feel good. Making you come until you can't come anymore."

I pull her closer until her pussy is plastered to my stomach. She still can't leverage herself to fuck me, but each little shake and shiver rubs her clit against me. I keep up the slow, thorough fucking as her breathing quickens and the sweet little pleasure sounds she's making become almost continuous. "That's right. Let go. There's no reason to deny yourself. We have all night, Grace. We're just getting started."

She comes hard, clenching on my fingers tightly enough that I curse. It's a good beginning. I don't give her time to recover before I tip her back on the bed and slide down between her thighs.

I've made a mess, and it's time to clean it up.

My first lick is pure paradise. Especially when she reaches down and grabs my horns. Again, she's not trying to guide the experience, she's hanging on while I give her what we both need. I start with long, thorough licks. I could spend days with my mouth on this woman's pussy. She's too fucking perfect. Sweet on my tongue and spread wide open to give me access to everything.

I tease her as long as I can hold out. Not nearly long enough, honestly. Maybe there will come a time when I'm not about to blow my load simply from being near her. Tonight's not the night. I finally give in to the tugging on my horns and move up to press the flat of my tongue against her clit. Her back bows, and her thighs clench around my head.

Not yet. First I need . . .

I press three fingers into her pussy as I keep up that stroke against her clit that has her dancing on the edge. Grace comes with a scream and damned near snaps my head off my shoulders. I have to muscle her legs wide so I can keep fucking her with my fingers, keep drawing out her orgasm until all the strength goes out of her limbs. It takes a very long time. I love every second of it.

Only when she is limp and panting do I move back up her body and brace myself over her. "Do you want my cock now, or should I keep eating you out? Because I could feast on your pussy for hours."

She blinks up at me, her gray eyes dazed. Distantly, I wonder if she's beyond words. I should know better. Grace snakes her hand between us before wrapping it around my cock as best she can. She licks her lips. "Later, if you want. I might die if I don't have you inside me right now."

I feel the same way. I brush her hand from my cock and wrap my fist around it. I was too worried about giving her exactly what she commanded last time we had sex. This time, I want to enjoy the sight of my broad head parting her pussy's lips. It seems impossible that she can fit me. I tease us both as I draw my cock up and down her center, soaking my head with her desire.

"Hold your thighs apart for me."

She fumbles to do it. I've never seen her so uncoordinated, and I drink in the sight, knowing I am the cause. Finally, Grace hooks the back of her knees around me and holds her legs wide. Only then do I press my cock to her entrance. Slowly. No matter how I've readied her, I need to go slowly.

I feed her the head of my cock and pause. The sight . . . I want to imprint it on the backs of my eyes, to remember this moment forever. Instead I press deeper. She moans at every ridge. It's too fucking good. Everything about this is too fucking good.

Finally, at long last, I seat myself fully inside her. And then I look up her body. Color flushes her pale skin. She has her eyes closed and her head thrown back as she moans. "Look at me, Grace."

Slowly, oh so slowly, she blinks her eyes open. Her lips

are parted, and I can't help but lean down and nip the bottom one. "Too much?"

"Just the right amount," she gasps.

"If it gets to be too much, tell me." I wait for her jerky nod to brace my hands on either side of her shoulders and begin to move. Last time, it felt so good, I thought the top of my head might explode, but Grace couldn't effectively withdraw completely. In this position, I can.

Slow, slow, slow.

It becomes a cadence in my head, a reminder that we dance on a precarious edge and to move too quickly might mean I hurt her. That's not what I want this to be about,. We've had plenty of rough things between us, sharp edges and harsher words. Right now, in my bed, I only want pleasure and . . .

Love.

Her pussy clenches around me with each withdrawal as if she wants to keep me inside her. It's the greatest agony I've ever experienced. I never want it to stop. Every time I thrust forward, her body welcomes me more easily. And still she holds herself open for me. Trusting me to not take this too far. Trusting me to make her feel good. Better than good.

"*Bram.*"

"Yes." I don't know what I'm answering, but I shift so I can catch her hip and press my thumb to her clit. I don't stroke—I think she's too sensitive for that at this point—but the movement of my thrusts rubs her against the pad of my thumb. Over and over and over. I grit my teeth, fighting against my body's instinct to fill her. I *need* her to come again. I need to feel it. I need to know it's for me and me alone.

Grace orgasms, and even though I was expecting it, the strength catches me by surprise. She drags me over the edge with her. I never stood a chance. I curse and surge forward, grinding into her pussy as I come and come and come. Filling her up. Overfilling her. I watch in helpless desire as my seed spills out around my cock and coats our thighs.

I gather her to me. I'm not sure if she's shaking, or if I am, or if we both are. It doesn't matter. Not when she's holding me to her just as hard. Grace buries her face in my chest and emits a breathless laugh. "Holy shit, Bram."

"We're not done yet."

Her next laugh is almost panicked. "The mind is willing, but I don't think my body can take any more. You're too big."

I grin against her hair. "I had a delivery during the time we weren't speaking. If the mind is willing . . . I have a solution for the body."

22

GRACE

I watch in fascination as Bram brings out a glass bottle and explains its purpose. Healing solution. It's used to facilitate humans fucking people who are much larger than them. Of course the bargainer demons came up with it. They have a vested interest in that sort of thing.

In the end, I only have one answer to the question on his face. "Yes. Again."

I am much sorer than I was last time. I watch with no small amount of trepidation as Bram coats his cock in the solution. I raise my brows. "It seems like there are better ways to apply it."

"There are." He lifts me into his lap so I'm facing away from him. I can't help but tense, yet the flicker of worry changes to pure pleasure as he gently saws his fingers through my folds. Almost instantly, the pain is gone, replaced by a lovely warmth. Bram's voice is rough in my ear. "When we're done, I'll use my fingers and make you come one last time to help you heal. But right now, you need my cock again, don't you?"

Yes. Desperately. As much as I like the games we've

played, tonight feels like it has changed everything. He's not holding me as if I'm priceless because I commanded him to. He's doing it because he truly feels like I'm priceless. I'm not riding his face because I want to tease him until he comes too quick . . . Well, maybe I was doing that a little bit. But I've never felt more cared for in my life. That's probably a sad thing to acknowledge, but it's hard to feel sad when Bram is lifting me onto his cock.

The earlier fucking and the healing solution ease the way. This time we don't have to fight for every inch. I'm able to wiggle my way down his length without too much trouble at all. And all the while, the ache fades. "I hope you bought the shit in bulk."

His laugh is strangled. "I have another order placed already." He wraps his arms around me, and then his wings follow, cutting off what little light there was in the room. Maybe this should feel claustrophobic, but I just feel protected.

We move slowly, the earlier frenzy having abated a little. I can feel it on the fringe, just waiting for the right spark to turn into an inferno once more. But for now . . . there's just lazy pleasure. I ride his cock as he holds me close. At some point I become aware that he's whispering in my ear, too softly for me to make out the words. I don't need to, though. His caring and tenderness are wrapped up in every piece of this experience.

If feels like love.

When I come, it's just as soft as everything else. But this time, Bram doesn't follow me over the edge. He topples me onto my stomach and covers me with his body, wedging one arm between my hips and the bed so he can lift me to slide deeper. His other hand slides down to cover my pussy and give me something to grind on. But he never picks up the pace. He doesn't withdraw more than absolutely necessary. The slow, dreamlike fucking brings me to the edge again and again. Only when I've lost all sense of time and place and anything but Bram does he allow himself to come again.

And it's perfect. Everything is perfect.

We don't stop for a very, very long time.

I lie in Bram's arms as the sweat cools on our bodies. It seems to take a lot longer than I would expect for my heart to ease back to a more normal pace. Maybe it never will. I rub my nose against Bram's chest and smile as he pulls me closer. This is what happiness feels like. I don't have an urge to be somewhere else, a pressure building and telling me that I'm not doing enough. I just . . . am. And that's perfect. That's all he expects of me.

I press a soft kiss to his pec. "My favorite color is purple. I don't own much of it because it's not practical; it stands out too much, draws the eye, which is exactly why it's something a hunter shouldn't wear. But I love it in all its frivolousness."

Bram trails his fingers down my spine. "I like pink." When I lift my head in surprise, he smiles. "Not hot pink. A deep rouge."

Understanding dawns in a slow wave. Hot pink is lust. But the color he's describing? That's love. I haven't had cause to see it much in my life. My grandparents didn't love me. They saw me as a tool to be used, an extension of their legacy. My parents did, but all too often that emotion was cast over in favor of other, harsher ones. "It's a beautiful color." It's one that . . . I'm seeing right now. I don't know how to process that. He hasn't said the words, but does he need to when I can see the truth written on his aura?

Do I when he can see the truth on mine?

"Yes, it is."

A truth I've kept close bubbles up inside me. "I'm part gargoyle. Or at least one of my ancestors was. I can read your energy just like you can read mine. I know what that color means."

"Thank you for telling me." He smooths my hair back. "I have no desire to hide anything from you, either. I'll tell you anything you want to know. Just ask."

There are so many things I want to know, but again I think back to his throwaway comment in his office about all the things we don't know about each other. "Will you tell me your family members' names? And more about them?"

Bram sucks in a harsh breath. "Yes, of course. Rae was one of the twins. They had just turned twenty-two. Practically a baby. They really loved sculpting and pottery. They were very good at it. Felix was the other twin, and he was the best hunter I've ever seen. He could also make anyone laugh with his ridiculous jokes." He trails off, and I almost cut in to tell him that he doesn't have to do this if he doesn't want to, but he continues speaking before I get a chance. "Amelia was only a year younger than me. She was a gigantic pain in my ass. Anything I did, she was quick to prove she could do better—and she *could* do it better. I don't know if she actually wanted to be ruler of this territory, but she likely would've been better at that too. She was smart and ambitious, and if she was a little asshole sometimes, I think that's just how siblings are."

My heart breaks for him. I don't know what it says about me that even in the midst of wishing he hadn't gone through such devastating loss, a part of me is still jealous that he had those relationships to begin with. I'm an only child. My mother was a hunter, and her pregnancy with me was not an easy one. She decided that the cost was too high, even if it meant I was the one who would have to worry about continuing the family legacy. When I was younger, I loved that I had my parents' sole attention. It was only as I grew older that the true cost and loneliness set in. I don't know how much of it is being an only child and the family legacy placed on me.

Bram keeps touching me, little strokes that are meant for comfort, though I don't know if he's comforting me or himself. "My father was Arthur. People say my mother was the great love of his life, but I don't think it's the truth. I don't know if he was even capable of love. He was always remote with us. I don't know if he was a bad man, but I don't think he was a good one. He claimed he brought the human in to increase the power in our territory, but I saw how he was with her. It was obsession, plain and simple. Selfish desire."

"The decision on whether to have children—and who to have them with—shouldn't be made because of power or family legacy. It should be made because you want a child and a family." The words feel ripped from my chest. Our histories are not the same, and neither are our circumstances, but I know all too well the hurt I've experienced being seen as a gear in the machine instead of a person in and of myself.

"You're right. It shouldn't. Even if he had been telling the truth about his motivation, it's still shitty of him. We don't have to live our lives like they did." Bram's heart is a steady beat against my cheek. "Will you tell me about your parents?"

It's the absolute least I can do. "My father's name was Gerald. He married into the family, but he took up hunting as if it were in his blood. Or at least that's what my mother used to say. He was killed by a werewolf when I was fourteen. The werewolf was terrorizing a small town, stealing the women from their beds. Dad cut off his head, but he dealt a mortal blow before Dad was able to finish him off." Killing that werewolf was an undeniably necessary thing to do. The human police were only half right when they thought they had a serial killer on their hands. Even if they'd managed to corner the culprit, he would've torn through them like wet tissue paper. Because werewolves have superior healing and ridiculously fast reflexes, the only way to be sure they are really dead is to decapitate them. Last I checked, cops weren't running around with swords and cutting off heads.

"I'm sorry."

I smile even though my eyes are burning. "We keep saying that to each other, over and over, for our pains that words won't fix."

"Sometimes there's nothing else to say."

He's right. Words might not change anything about our past, but words are all we have right now. I take a deep breath. "My mother grew up the same as me. Trained from birth to kill. Except not really the same as me at all. My father was a balancing force. He didn't have the old prejudices my grandfather did. He wouldn't go on a hunt unless it was proven that the monster he was hunting had harmed a human. When my mother married him, she adopted that policy as well. But when he died, things went a little strange. My grandfather only lived another year after my father, though it was disease that got him rather than violence. Ironic, that. But my mother started searching for something, some kind of answer to a question that I still don't know. She was driven to the point of obsession. She disappeared the year I turned twenty. I've been searching for answers for five years, but I've never been able to find out *why*. That's why I came here." I exhale shakily. "Sorry, I'm getting ahead of myself. My mother's name was Barbara."

Bram freezes. It's as if he's turned to stone next to me, his arms no longer a comforting embrace but instead a cage. "What did you say?"

The movies and storybooks like to pretend that when something terrible happens, it happens in slow motion. Life is rarely that kind. Understanding, when it comes, happens in an instant. Pieces click together, and I wonder why I never saw it before. Why did I never question the details of his history, Azazel's hesitance, Ramanu's careful handling of us? I should have.

When Bram speaks, I already know the words before they reach the air between us. "Barbara was the name of the human who killed my family."

23

BRAM

I don't shove Grace away from me, even though every instinct I have is demanding I put space between us. Instead, I gently nudge her aside and climb out of the bed. It's still not enough distance between us.

I should've put the pieces together earlier. I knew Grace said she saved people, but so many times saving oneperson means killing another. That's the truth lay in the margins of her silence. Which means her mother did the same thing; her mother, who made a demon bargain some time ago and was never seen again. How likely would it be that her missing mother and the human who killed my family weren't connected? The odds that they were are astronomical. And yet I never questioned it.

Maybe because I didn't want to.

"I need to go. I need to think."

"Bram, wait!" To her credit, she doesn't leave the bed or try to approach me. She also doesn't clutch the sheet to her naked chest or pretend to be anything other than what she is. A predator. The way she watches me . . . if I attacked her now, she would meet me, violence for violence. She wouldn't hesitate. Grace swallows visibly. I can barely think clearly enough to process the riot of color in her energy. "Can we please just talk about this?"

Her mother is responsible for the death of everyone I've ever loved. Even knowing that Grace didn't come here for the same purpose, how does someone move past a hurt like this? Some mountains are too high to fly over. "What is there to say?" I laugh, the sound harsh in my throat. "Maybe my people are right. Maybe my family is cursed. I can think of no other explanation for me finding the person my soul connects to most, only to discover the body of violence that means we can never be together."

"Bram." Grace still hasn't moved. It's like she thinks that if she shifts too quickly, she'll drive me from the room. I'm not sure she's wrong. "This is a shock for me, too. I don't . . ." She shakes her head and lifts her chin. "Please don't say anything that you can't take back. I've meant every single word I've said to you. I care about you. Hell, I'm falling for you. I have set aside my entire purpose for being here in order to spend more time with you. I know this is fucked up—"

"Fucked up," I echo. "Fucked up doesn't begin to cover it. I just summoned the nobles to this castle. What do you think they will do when they find out I have the daughter of the monster who killed my family, in my bed, willingly? They won't follow me. I can't even blame them for that."

Grace's eyes seem too large in her face, her pale skin blanched. "That's what you're concerned about?"

I don't know what I'm concerned about. I don't know what I'm feeling. I should've seen this coming, and the humiliation that I didn't is almost too much to bear. Azazel knew. Ramanu too. Were they laughing at me behind my back? Poor, foolish Bram, too shortsighted to realize he had an enemy in his midst. And "fool" doesn't begin to cover the fact that I have fallen in love with this woman.

I don't know how to reconcile how I feel about her against everything that now stands between us. "I need time."

"I don't know a single person who said they need time who has ever come back."

I don't either. It's usually the beginning of the end. "I need time," I repeat. "You wanted answers from Azazel. I'll send you back to the bargainer demon territory to get them. After I meet with the nobles here, we'll talk."

"Sure we will. Whatever you say." The fire inside Grace is dampened. She's being bathed in the pale blue of sorrow threaded with the violet of resolve. I watch in silence as she stands and pulls on her clothes. This feels like the worst goodbye I've ever had to say, and I don't know how to stop it. I do need time. But I don't know if it will result in me talking myself into being with her . . . or out of being with her.

Grace stops in front of me, and for one breathless moment, I think that she's going to tell me she loves me. I saw that color in her energy earlier. I know I did. Instead she stares at the center of my chest. "I would like to leave the room."

And I'm standing in her way.

I step to the side, and she walks past me without another word. I tell myself to go after her, to tell her that it doesn't matter what the past holds because we choose the future. I don't move an inch. Not until I'm sure she's gone back to her room. Only then do I fly to my study and pen a summons to Ramanu. I'm not ready to face Azazel yet. Maybe I never will be.

No, that's a coward's thinking. I will face Azazel. I will certainly ask him why he chose to send Grace to me. Yes, he protested, but not that strongly, and he never told me why. It's almost enough for me to think . . . I shake my head sharply. Grace is no assassin sent to kill me. I may not be certain of much, but I am certain of that. This situation is fucked up but not that fucked up.

I write the summons, and it's only a few seconds later when Ramanu arrives. They walk through my door as if they arrived here by mundane means instead of teleportation. "You called?" Their tone is irreverent, but their energy gives them away.

"Why are you worried, Ramanu? Is it possibly because Grace is the daughter of the woman who killed my entire family?"

They eye me, and their shoulders drop several inches. "In my defense, I already told you that I argued against it."

"Yes, you said you were against it . . . but not why." I turn away. "Take her."

"Excuse me?"

"Was I not clear? I don't want Grace here right now. If I change my mind, I will come retrieve her."

Ramanu is silent for so long, my curiosity and frustration override my good sense and I turn to face them. They are studying me with a strange look on their face. "You love her." I don't feel like they're laughing at me. "Why are you sending her away if that's how you feel?"

We are not friends. We never will be. But in this moment, I give them honesty when I can barely be honest with myself. "It's because I love her that I'm sending her away. I don't know if there's a path forward for us through this, but there definitely isn't if I don't have time and space to work through this revelation. I don't want to hurt her while I'm in pain."

"I see." They nod. "Very well. When you come to retrieve her, send a warning to us."

I don't know whether to be grateful or frustrated that they have no doubt I will come for Grace. But then, they're right, aren't they? I might not see a path through, but I didn't see myself getting to this place either. There has to be a way. But I can barely think past the betrayal and pain wrapped around my throat.

Her *mother*.

The specter that haunts my nightmares, who left her fingerprints on all my trauma, is the woman who birthed Grace. The mother who taught her everything she knows. The one Grace loved enough to search for by bargaining away seven years of her life in a realm filled with monsters like the ones she spent her life hunting. They are the same person, and I don't know how to reconcile that. I don't know if it's possible.

I swear I sense the moment Ramanu takes Grace from the castle. It shouldn't be possible to feel her absence with this much space between us, but I do. I'm sure of it. I don't know if I'm making a mistake. I don't know anything at all.

Days pass without answers. It doesn't matter what path my thoughts travel; they all end up in the same place. Grace and I were doomed from the start. No matter what our intentions were, the circumstances are simply impossible. Fuck if that doesn't hurt, a new scar to add to my collection. I don't know how to be with her, but if I can't figure it out, I'm going to spend the rest of my life missing her.

It's almost a week to the day when there's a rough knock

on the door to my study. I know who's on the other side. There's only one person in this realm whose energy constantly has the deep forest green of pride. It's aggravating enough even without my current circumstances. "Come in." I might as well get this over with.

Azazel steps into my study and looks around. He's as out of place here as a hellcat in water, but somehow that doesn't seem to bother him. He's never lacking in confidence. "I thought we should speak."

"Oh, are we speaking now? Or would you like to continue to withhold vital information from me?"

He smiles but not like anything is funny. "You're starting to sound like her."

Her. Grace. I want to snap at him to not talk about her, but there's only one reason for him to be here, and it's to talk about Grace. "You should've told me."

"I know." He motions to the chair across my desk. "May I sit?"

I could keep up this posturing, but what's the point? We need to have this conversation, one way or another. "Sure."

I study him as he does so. Even here, in the study of someone who could be an enemy, he's perfectly at ease. This is a man who knows his place in the world. I can't help a flicker of jealousy. It's comforting, at least, to know that he can't read my energy the way Ramanu can.

Azazel's powers lie in a different direction.

"I made the deal with Barbara Jaeger for my own purposes, but I honestly didn't think she would be a danger to your family. She consented to spend her time with your father as his consort. I had no reason to believe she was being anything but genuine. In hindsight, I should've questioned it more, but I was new to my throne and needed the alliance enough to be a little desperate. I'm not excusing my negligence. I'm merely explaining how we got to that place."

"I'm aware." As much as I would love to blame Azazel for the entire situation, every other action he's taken since gaining leadership of his territory proves that he is a fair and generous leader intent on peace.

He studies me long enough for it to become uncomfortable. "Grace is not her mother. She might've agreed to pay the price of seven years because she thought she'd get answers, but ultimately she did it for the benefit of someone she barely knew. I kept tabs on her after things went so poorly with Barbara. I suppose I felt guilty for depriving a daughter of her mother. Grace is ruthless, but she's also fair and kind to those weaker than herself."

"You're not telling me anything I don't already know. I recognized her from the first true conversation we had, and nothing that has happened in the meantime has dissuaded me."

He narrows his eyes. "If that's the case, then why is she terrorizing my household instead of yours?"

My frustration and anger bloom inside of me, hot and sticky and overwhelming. "You understand the circumstances around my family's death were orchestrated by a single person. I am still working to understand that. My people don't. What do you think will happen when they realize the woman at my side and in my bed is the daughter of the very same one who enacted the so-called curse they believe in so strongly?"

"So prove them wrong."

I blink. "Excuse me?"

"You know what my predecessor was like. She encouraged cruelty and rewarded violence. The culture she fostered didn't simply go away when I took the throne. I have spent years weeding out the poisonous garden she planted. I won't lie and tell you it's been an easy task or even one that most of my people truly appreciate or notice. But can you look me in the face and tell me things haven't changed under my roof?"

No, I can't tell him that. Things *have* changed. Not only in the demon bargainer territory, but in the rest of the realm. His leadership, and the line he drew in the sand, created ripples over every other territory. His pursuit of peace has dragged all of us along behind. He's not the sole one responsible for said peace, but he is an incredible influence. "You never faltered?"

"Of course I faltered. I've doubted myself. I've questioned whether this was all fruitless. The difference is that I never let that show out in the open. Your people won't change overnight, Bram. But if you give them hope, a good portion of them will move into a new future with you."

Hope is a strange thing. Until my time with Grace, I didn't have much of it at all. Now Azazel wants me to teach hope to my people. I'm not sure it's even possible, but I can't deny that his territory was in significantly worse shape when he took over. He and I are not the same, though.

Azazel sighs. "I won't lie to you. It's a lonely road. I didn't have anyone at my side who believed in me and my vision. So I had to believe enough for everyone. Of course I fucking doubted myself, Bram. It was an impossible task, and I'm not through with it yet." He pushes slowly to his feet. "From what I can tell, you wouldn't be doing it alone. That's something you should think about."

I have spent so long feeling helpless against the whims of my people that the idea of pushing back is one I've barely put into action. I wouldn't have at all if not for Grace. I suppose that means Azazel is right. I'm not alone. Unless I fucked things up beyond repair. "Azazel."

"Yeah?"

"Tell Grace I'm coming for her tomorrow. If she still wants to see me."

"Bram." He looks over his shoulder at me, expression grim. "If you don't come for her tomorrow, *she's* liable to come looking for *you*."

24

GRACE

I should be happy to be back in the bargainer demon castle.

It's where I wanted to get originally, after all.

The answers I've sought for so long are here.

Too bad every single one of those thoughts rings hollow now. I know what happened to my mother. She killed an entire family and then was probably sentenced to death. I wish I could say I don't understand why she would make that choice, but in the days since Bram sent me away, bits and pieces of the past have settled into place like a puzzle I can finally see in full.

After my father died, the teachings of my grandfather crept in around the edges. I was only fourteen. Too young to realize the poison infecting my mother's mind. But now, with the hindsight of true adulthood, it's all too clear. It's enough to make me wonder why I didn't see it before. Except I know the answer to that, don't I?

I didn't want to see it.

Azazel was right. There's no satisfaction in this. Instead of feeling relief from the knowledge, all I can do is worry that I'll never see Bram again. How can he stand to look at me, knowing I'm related to the reason he suffered so much loss?

Misery is a cloak I wear wrapped around every inch of my skin. I wander the castle for hours, for days. No one bothers me. Even the castle itself seems to take pity on me. It routes me through the kitchen at regular intervals to ensure I eat. Another time, that might amuse me. Right now, there's no room for amusement.

I've gotten so used to being alone that when the castle spits me out into a room instead of another hallway, it takes me several long seconds to realize I'm not by myself. I'm in a study with a dark color scheme and an oversized desk that looks like it's made of rock. Behind that desk sits Azazel. He looks a little different from the last time I saw him. Tired. The lines around his mouth and eyes are deeper than before. Exhaustion weighs heavy in his aura, dimming its colors. Maybe that shit should please me, but I'm so gods-damned tired of suffering in all its forms. "You look like shit."

"Thanks." He gives a wan smile. "You're not looking so hot yourself. Since you're back, I thought it was time we have a conversation that you've been seeking."

Again, the relief I expected to feel is nowhere in evidence. I drop into one of the chairs across from him. "I don't know what else there is to say. I know she killed Bram's family. I can even guess why."

"She didn't just kill his family." Azazel says it so gently, it takes a bit for the words to penetrate. "After she left the castle, we couldn't find her. Not until she showed up in the incubus and succubus territory and killed several of their high-ranking members. Rusalka was able to restrain her and bring her to me, and upon questioning, I discovered that she had every intention of killing her way through all the leadership positions in this realm."

I wish I could say I'm surprised. But this was clearly a suicide mission. Sorrow weighs me down. What a fucked-up family I come from. "That sounds like something my grandfather would do."

"He tried to make deals with my predecessor several times. I expect that was his plan all along, which he obviously communicated to your mother at some point." He watches me closely. If there were pity in his aura, I don't know what I would do. But there's just a gentle understanding in a shared sorrow. "Bram isn't aware of the other damage she did. Rusalka wanted to keep it internal, and I respected her wishes. You're the only person outside her territory—and me—who is aware of it."

I appreciate his candor, and as much as part of me feels that it's too little too late, knowing the truth earlier would have meant that I wouldn't have had a chance to know Bram. It's so selfish of me to be grateful for the time we spent together, even if it was limited, even if it hurt us both. I don't care. "What did my mother ask for? As her bargain?"

Azazel leans back, his expression unreadable. "She asked for protection for you."

"Excuse me?"

"It was limited. I'm not a celestial, capable of blessing someone across every facet of their life. But we bargainer demons have many spells and even more variety of magic. You haven't been sick since you were a teenager, have you? And you heal faster than you have any right to. I couldn't guarantee your protection, but I was able to stack the deck in your favor. Your training and your instincts have done the rest."

It feels like he kicked the chair right out from underneath me. I don't know how to feel. My mother was a monster, and what she did was unforgivable. But . . . she loved me. No matter what else is true, that is. I rub my chest, trying to ease the tightness there. "This is a lot."

"Yes. Be gentle with yourself while you process it. I expect you'll feel a wide range of emotions, and none of them are incorrect."

That draws a sharp laugh from me. "Are you a therapist now, Azazel?"

"I know you'd prefer to see me as the orchestrator of all your ills, but I take the protection and care of my humans incredibly seriously. That includes your mental health. If you want to talk to someone, I have several qualified people on staff. That's an open-ended offer, by the way. You don't have to answer now."

I would've thought that by now my capacity for feeling surprise would be exhausted. And yet here I am, being offered therapy by a demon. Part of me wants to turn him down flat, but that's just my hurt talking. "I'll think about it. Seems like I'll be in proximity for the next six years and change, so there's plenty of time."

"About that. I don't expect you'll be in the castle nearly that long." He ignores my questioning look and motions to the door behind me—a clear indication that this meeting is over. "Why don't you take a walk and get some fresh air? The castle will show you the way. "

There's no point in arguing. If I need Azazel, I know where to find him, more or less. And he's right; I could use some fresh air.

I'm not sure how I reach the roof without taking a single set of stairs. Magic is strange like that; it seems the castle took pity on me once again. I try not to think about it too hard. Bars crisscross in a gorgeous iron pattern overhead, no doubt designed to keep the winged monsters at bay. The sky is clear right now, though. It's a cool day, and this high up, the wind whips at my clothing. I wish I could scour away my conflicted feelings. But that's not how life works.

I miss Bram. I feel absolutely foolish for letting my anger get the best of me and keep me apart from him for the last week I was there. All those days spent exploring his castle, I could've spent with him. At least then I would have more memories to shore me up through the rest of my life. He said he needed time and space, but surely that time and space will spotlight how much he doesn't want to be with the daughter of a murderer.

Not even just the daughter of a murderer, but the murderer who *killed Bram's family*.

I'm so wrapped up in my thoughts that I think I've hallucinated the feeling of Bram's eyes on me. Then the door opens behind me, and the man himself steps out onto the roof.

I have to plant my feet in order not to throw myself into his arms. I don't know why he's here. I can't afford to assume it's good news. I do my best to filter out the colors of his aura because I'm too afraid to see the truth there. "Bram."

"Grace." He looks away and then immediately back at me, as if he can't bear to have me out of sight. I feel the same. I'm drinking in the sight of him, working hard to memorize every little detail. His wings shift restlessly. "I've had some time to think."

I brace myself. This is the moment when he ends things for good. Trust Bram to make the trip to do it in person. No matter what else is true, he's not nearly the coward he thinks he is. "Okay."

He searches my face for several long moments. I don't know what he finds there. I don't know what to think or how to feel right now. This is the moment. He will open his mouth and let me down as gently as possible. And then I will have to move forward and figure out how to pick up the pieces yet again.

"I love you."

I stare. Did he just say what I think he just said? "What?"

"It won't be easy to be with me. Things in my territory are a mess, and that's not going to change anytime soon. The nobles will push back against any change I make. They will try to incentivize you to leave, and when they realize that won't work—you were right—they'll try to hurt you. But someone very wise told me that hope is a powerful thing. I think, with you by my side, we can give that to my people. If it all goes terribly wrong and they oust me from the throne, at least we'll be together." He swallows visibly. "If you want to, I mean."

I blink several times, still trying to keep up with the direction the conversation has gone. "But my mother—"

"You're not your mother. Just like I'm not my father. It's not fair to judge each other by those standards. I . . ." He shakes his head. "I'm not saying it's not going to be a problem once the truth of your family comes out. And I can't pretend those old hurts won't rise from time to time to sting us. No matter what else is true, it's going to be a lot of work to step out of the long shadows our parents cast. But I have to believe we can do it."

Hope hits me so intensely, I'm surprised I don't rise right off the roof of the castle. "You love me."

"Yeah. I love you." He grins suddenly. "It's written all over my energy if you care to look."

My eyes are burning, and I have a hard time swallowing past the lump in my throat. "I don't have to test you, Bram. You said you love me, and I believe you." I press my lips together hard, as if that would be enough to still their trembling. "What happens now?"

Bram extends his hand slowly. "I'd like you to come home with me. I'd like you to move into my room permanently. And, in a few weeks, when all the nobles gather, I'd like you to stand at my side as I address them."

I start to reach for his hand but pause. "But I'm only in the demon realm for seven years."

"Maybe." He doesn't move. "I know it's possible to stay after the contract is fulfilled, but why don't we take it day by day?"

I appreciate him giving me the time and space to make that decision, but I have a feeling that ship already sailed for me. I wait for guilt to rise at the thought of leaving behind my family legacy, of no longer being a hunter, but all I feel is overwhelming relief. As if I've set down heavy weight I've been carrying for longer than I can possibly remember. I don't know what the future holds, but when I step forward into Bram's arms, hope is the overwhelming emotion lifting me even as he sweeps me up. "I love you, too, you know."

"I know." Bram gathers me close and brushes gentle kisses to my lips. "But I'll spend the rest of my life never getting tired of hearing you say it."

"Then I'll say it again." I kiss him. "I love you."

ABOUT THE AUTHOR

Katee Robert is a *New York Times* and USA Today bestselling author of spicy romance. *Entertainment Weekly* calls her writing "unspeakably hot." Her books have sold over two million copies. She lives in the Pacific Northwest with her husband, children, a cat who thinks he's a dog, and two Great Danes who think they're lap dogs.

www.kateerobert.com

Printed in the USA
CPSIA information can be obtained
at www.ICGtesting.com
LVHW030820130923
757986LV00006B/556